So Much Blood

So Much Blood

Simon Brett

Charles Scribner's Sons
NEW YORK

CHAPTER ONE

My brain is dull my sight is foul,
I cannot write a verse, or read—
Then, Pallas, take away thine Owl,
And let us have a Lark instead.

TO MINERVA—FROM THE GREEK

'MAURICE SKELLERN ARTISTES,' said the voice that answered the telephone.

'Maurice—'

'Who wants him?'

'Maurice, for God's sake. I know it's you. Why you always have to go through this rigmarole of pretending you've got a staff of thousands, I don't know. It's me—Charles.'

'Ah, hello. Pity about the telly series.'

'Yes, it would have been nice.'

'And good money, Charles.'

'Yes. Still, in theory it's only been postponed. Till this P.A.s' strike is over.'

'When will that be, though?'

'Don't know.'

'What is a P.A. anyway? I can never understand all that B.B.C. hierarchy. Do you know what a P.A. is?'

'Vaguely.' Charles Paris had a feeling that a P.A. was either a Production Assistant or a Producer's Assistant, but his knowledge of the breed was limited to an erotic night in Fulham with a girl called Angela after recording an episode of *Dr Who*. And they had not discussed the anomalies of the P.A.s' conditions of service that led to the strike which in August 1974 was crippling B.B.C. Television's Drama and Light Entertainment Departments. 'Anything else on the horizon, Maurice?'

7

'Had an enquiry from the Haymarket, Leicester. Might want you to direct a production of . . .' he paused, '. . . the Head Gabbler?'

'Hedda Gabler?'

'That's it.'

'Could be fun. When?'

'Not till the spring.'

'Great.' Heavy sarcasm.

'Might be a small part in a film. Playing a German football manager.'

'Oh yes?'

'But that's very vague.'

'Terrific. Listen, Maurice, I've got something.'

'Getting your own work, eh?'

'Somebody's got to.'

'Ooh, that hurt, Charles. I try, you know, I try.'

'Yes. My heart bleeds, an agent's lot is not a happy one, mournful violin plays *Hearts and Flowers*. No, it's for *So Much Comic, So Much Blood.*'

'What?'

'You know, my one-man show on Thomas Hood. Thing I did for the York Festival and the British Council recitals.'

'Oh yes.' The tone of Maurice's voice recalled the tiny fees of which he had got ten per cent.

'A friend of mine, guy I knew in Oxford who now lectures in the Drama Department at Derby University, has offered me a week at the Edinburgh Festival. Some show's fallen through, one the students were doing, and they're desperate for something cheap to fill the lunchtime slot. Just for a week.'

'Charles, how many times do I have to tell you, you mustn't ever take something cheap? It's not official Festival, is it?'

'No, on the Fringe. I get fifty per cent of box office.'

'Fifty per cent of box office on a lunchtime show on the Fringe of the Edinburgh Festival won't buy you a pair of socks. There's no point in doing it, Charles. You're better off down here. A voice-over for a commercial might come up, or a radio. Edinburgh'll cost you, anyway. Fares, accommodation.'

'I get accommodation.'

'But, Charles, you've got to ask yourself, is it the right thing for you to be doing, artistically?' Maurice made this moving appeal every time Charles suggested something unprofitable.

'I don't know. It's a long time since I've been to Edinburgh.'

'Charles, take my advice. Don't do it.'

As he emerged from Waverley Station, Charles Paris sniffed the caramel hint of breweries in the air and felt the elation which Edinburgh always inspired in him. It is, he thought, a theatrical city. The great giant's castle looms stark against the cyclorama, and from it the roofs of the Royal Mile tumble down a long diagonal. There are so many levels, like a brilliant designer's stage set. Plenty of opportunities for the inventive director. The valley of Princes Street, with a railway instead of a river and the Victorian kitsch of the Scott Memorial instead of an imposing centrepiece, is ideal for ceremonial entrances. From there, according to the play, the director can turn to the New Town or the Old. The New Town is designed for comedy of manners. Sedate, right-angled, formal, George Street and Queen Street, regularly intersected and supported by the tasteful bookends of Charlotte and Saint Andrew Squares, stand as Augustan witnesses to the Age of Reason.

The director should use the Old Town for earthier drama, scenes of low life. It is a tangle of interweaving streets, wynds and steps, ideal settings for murder and mystery, with a thousand dark corners to hide stage thugs. This is the city of Burke and Hare, of crime and passion.

The Old Town made Charles think of Melissa, an actress who had been in a show with him at the Lyceum fifteen

9

years before. After a disastrous three months he had returned to London and his wife Frances, but Melissa had made Edinburgh seem sexy, like a prim nanny shedding her grey uniform behind the bushes in the park.

On Sunday 11th August 1974 the city still felt sexy. And this time Charles Paris was free. He had left Frances in 1962.

Everything smelt fresh after recent rain. Charles felt vigorous, younger than his forty-seven years. He decided to walk. Frances would have caught a bus; she had an uncanny ability for comprehending any bus system within seconds of arrival in a town. Charles would walk. He set off, swinging his holdall like a schoolboy. The only shadow on his sunny mood was the fact that Scottish pubs are closed on Sundays.

He couldn't miss the house in Coates Gardens. Among the self-effacing homes and hotels of the Edinbourgeois there was one whose pillars and front door were plastered with posters.

D.U.D.S. ON THE FRINGE!
Derby University Dramatic Society presents
*FOUR WORLD PREMIÈRES!
ONE GREAT CLASSIC!
A Midsummer Night's Dream—Shakespeare's Immortal Comedy Revisualised by Stella Galpin-Lord.
Mary, Queen of Sots—a Mixed-Media Satire of Disintegration by Sam Wasserman.
Isadora's Lovers—Lesley Petter's Examination of a Myth in Dance and Song.
Who Now?—a Disturbing New Play by Martin Warburton.
Brown Derby—Simply the Funniest Late-Night Revue on the Fringe.

There followed lists of dates, times and prices for this complicated repertoire, from which Charles deduced that the show he was replacing was *Isadora's Lovers*. For some reason Lesley Petter was unable to Examine the Myth in Dance and Song. He felt annoyed that the poster had not been amended to advertise *So Much Comic, So Much Blood*. They had known he was coming for more than a week. And publicity is enormously important when you're competing with about two hundred and fifty other shows.

The doorbell immediately produced a plain, roly-poly girl in irrevocably paint-spattered jeans.

'Hello, I'm Charles Paris.'

'Oh Lord, how exciting, yes. I'm Pam Northcliffe, Props. Just zooming down to the hall to make the axe for *Mary*. Going to build it round this.' She waved a squeezy washing-up liquid bottle. 'So the blood spurts properly.'

'Ah.'

'Brian's in the office. Through there.' She scurried off down the road, bouncing like a beach-ball.

The shining paint on the partitions of the hall was evidence that the house had only recently been converted into flats. The door marked 'Office' in efficient Letraset was ajar. Inside it was tiny, the stub-end of a room unaccounted for in the conversion plans. A young man in a check shirt and elaborate tie was busy on the telephone. He airily indicated a seat.

'Look, I know it's the weekend, I know you're working every hour there is. So are we. It's just got to be ready. Well, what time tomorrow? No, earlier than that. Midday . . .'

The wrangle continued. Charles looked at a large baize-covered board with the optimistic Letraset heading, 'What the Press says about D.U.D.S.' So far the Press had not said much, which was hardly surprising, because the Festival did not begin for another week. In the middle of the board was one cutting. A photograph of a girl, and underneath it :

UNDERSTUDY STEPS IN

It's an ill wind, they say, and it's certainly blown some good the way of Derby University Dramatic Society's Anna Duncan. When one of the group's actresses Lesley Petter broke her leg in an accident last week, suddenly

20-year-old Anna found she was playing two leading rôles —in a play and a revue, both to be seen at the Masonic Hall in Lauriston Street when the Festival starts. Says Anna, 'I'm really upset for poor Lesley's sake, but it's a wonderful chance for me. I'm very excited.' And with lovely Anna onstage, Fringe-goers may get pretty excited too!

The reporter, whatever his shortcomings in style, was right about one thing. Even in the blurred photograph the girl really was lovely. She was pictured against the decorative railings of Coates Gardens. Slender body, long legs in well-cut jeans, a firm chin and expertly cropped blonde hair.

The telephone conversation finished and Charles received a busy professional handshake. 'I'm Brian Cassells, Company Manager.'

'Charles Paris.'

'I recognised you. So glad you could step in at such short notice. Nice spread, that.' He indicated the cutting. 'Helps having a pretty girl in the group. Important, publicity.'

'Yes,' said Charles.

The edge in his voice was not lost on Brian Cassells. 'Sorry about yours. That's what I was on to the printer about. Posters and handouts ready tomorrow.'

'Good. Did you get the stuff I sent up? The cuttings and so on.'

'Yes. Incorporated some in the poster. They were very good.'

Yes, thought Charles, they were good. He particularly cherished the one from the *Yorkshire Post*. 'There are many pleasures to be had at the York Festival, and the greatest of these is Charles Paris' *So Much Comic, So Much Blood.*'

The Company Manager moved hastily on, as if any pause or small talk might threaten his image of efficiency. 'Look, I'll show you the sleeping arrangements and so on.'

'Thanks. When will I be able to get into the hall to do some rehearsal?'

12

'It's pretty tied up tomorrow. Stella's having a D.R. of the *Dream*. Then Mike's in with *Mary*. That's Tuesday morning. Tuesday afternoon should be O.K. Just a photo-call for *Mary*. A few dramatic shots of Rizzio's murder, that sort of thing, good publicity. Shouldn't take long.'

The sleeping arrangements were spartan. The ground-floor rooms were filled with rows of ex-army camp-beds for the men, with the same upstairs for the girls. No prospects of fraternisation. 'It's not on moral grounds,' said Brian, 'just logistical. Kitchen and dining-room in the basement if you want a cup of coffee or something. I'd better get back. Got to do some Letrasetting.'

Charles dumped his case on a vacant camp-bed which wobbled ominously. The room had the stuffy smell of male bodies. It brought back National Service, the first dreary barracks he'd been sent to in 1945, to train for a war that was over before he was trained. He opened a window and enjoyed the relief of damp-scented air.

He felt much more than forty-seven as he sat over skinny coffee in the basement, surrounded by blue denim. An epicene couple were wrapped round each other on the sofa. A plump girl was relaxing dramatically on the floor. Three young men with ringlets were hunched over the table discussing The Theatre.

'What it's got to do is reflect society, and if you've got a violent society, then it's got to reflect that.'

The reply came back in a slightly foreign accent. German? Dutch? 'Bullshit, Martin. It's more complex than that. The Theatre interprets events. Like when I'm directing something, I don't just want to reflect reality. Not ordinary reality. I try to produce a new reality.'

Charles winced as the other took up the argument. 'What is reality, though? I reckon if people are getting their legs blown off in Northern Ireland, if they're starving in Ethiopia, you've got to show that. Even if it means physically assaulting the audience to get them to react.'

13

'So where is the violence, Martin? Onstage? In the audience?'

'It's everywhere. It's part of twentieth-century living. And we've got to be aware of that. Even, if necessary, be prepared to be violent ourselves, in a violent society. That's what my play's about.'

'That, Martin, is so much crap.'

The youth called Martin flushed, stood up and looked as if he was about to strike his opponent. Then the spasm passed and, sulkily, he left the room. Charles deduced he must be Martin Warburton, author of *Who Now?* a Disturbing New Play.

The other ringletted youth looked round for someone else to argue with. 'You're Charles Paris, aren't you?'

'Yes.'

'What do you think about violence in the theatre?'

'There's a place for it. It can make a point.' Charles knew he sounded irretrievably middle-aged.

The youth snorted. 'Yes, hinted at and glossed over in West End comedies.'

Charles was riled. He did not like being identified exclusively with the safe commercial theatre. His irritant continued. 'I'm directing *Mary, Queen of Sots*. That's got violence in perspective. Lots of blood.' He turned on Charles suddenly. 'You ever directed anything?'

'Yes.' With some warmth. 'In the West End and most of the major reps in the country.'

'Oh.' *Mary, Queen of Sots'* director was unimpressed. 'What, long time ago?'

'No, quite recently.' Charles' anger pushed him on. 'In fact I'm currently considering a production of *Hedda Gabler* at the new Haymarket Theatre in Leicester.'

'Big deal.' The ringletted head drooped forward over a Sunday newspaper.

Without making too much of a gesture of it, Charles left the room. In the hall he checked with a D.U.D.S. programme for details of his antagonist.

MICHAEL VANDERZEE—After work in experimental theatre in Amsterdam and in Munich under Kostbach, he made his directorial debut in this country with *Abusage* by Dokke at the Dark Brown Theatre. He has been responsible for introducing into this country the works of Schmiss and Turzinski, and recently directed the latter's *Ideas Towards a Revolution of the Audience* at the Theatre Upstairs. Drawing inspiration from the physical disciplines and philosophies of East and West, he creates a theatre indissolubly integrated with working life.

'Huh,' said Charles to himself. As he started towards his dormitory, a key turned in the front door lock and a middle-aged man in a sandy tweed suit appeared. He smiled and extended his hand. 'Hello, you must be Charles Paris.'

'Yes.'

'I'm James Milne, known to the students as the Laird. I live in the flat on the top floor. Would you like to come up for a drink?'

It was the most welcome sentence Charles had heard since he arrived. Edinburgh regained its charm.

'Yes, I agree. I am an unlikely person to be involved with Derby University Dramatic Society. It's a coincidence. I've only moved into this house recently and I sold my previous one in Meadow Lane to a lad called Willy Mariello. Have you met him yet?'

'No.'

'No doubt you will. He's with this lot. Well, the conversion here was more or less finished, but the summer's not a good time to get permanent tenants—holidays, the Festival and so on. So when Willy said this crowd was looking for somewhere, I offered it for the six weeks.'

'Brave.'

'I don't know. They pay rent. There's no furniture, not much they can break. And they've sworn they'll clean everything up before they go. I just hurry in and out and don't dare look at the mess.'

'What about noise?'

'This flat's pretty well insulated.'

'Largely by books, I should imagine. And this has only just been converted too? I can't believe it.'

The Laird glowed. Obviously Charles had said the right thing. But the flat did seem as if it had been there for centuries. Brown velvet upholstery and the leather spines of books gave the quality of an old sepia photograph. A library, an eyrie at the top of the building, it reminded Charles of his tutorials at Oxford. Dry sherry and dry donnish jokes. True, the sherry was malt whisky, but there was something of the don about James Milne.

'You like books?' He half-rose from his chair, eager, waiting for the slightest encouragement.

Charles gave it. 'Yes.'

'They're not first editions or anything like that. Well, not many of them. Just good editions. I do hate this paperback business. Some of the Dickens are quite good. And that *Vanity Fair* is valuable . . .'

Charles wondered if he was about to receive a lecture on antiquarian books, but the danger passed. '. . . and this edition of Scott might be worth something. Though not to the modern reader. Nobody reads him nowadays. I wonder why. Could it be because he's a dreary old bore? I think it must be. Even we Scots find him a bit of a penance.' He laughed. A cosy-looking man; probably mid-fifties, with a fuzz of white hair and bushy black eyebrows.

Charles laughed, too. 'I've read half of *Ivanhoe*. About seven times. Like *Ulysses* and the first volume of Proust. Never get any further.' He relaxed into his chair. 'It's very comforting, all those books.'

'Yes. "No furniture is so charming as books, even if you never open them or read a single word." The Reverend Sydney Smith. Not a Scot himself, but for some time a

16

significant luminary of Edinburgh society. Yes, my books are my life.'

Charles smiled. 'Wasn't it another Edinburgh luminary, Robert Louis Stevenson, who said, "Books are all very well in their way, but they're a mighty bloodless substitute for real life"?'

James Milne chuckled with relish, which was a relief to Charles, who was not sure that he had got the quotation right. 'Excellent, Charles, excellent, though the point is arguable. Let me give you a refill.'

It turned out that the Laird had been a schoolmaster at Kilbruce, a large public school just outside Edinburgh. 'I retired from there some five years ago. No, no, I'm not as old as all that. But when my mother died I came into some money and property—this house, an estate called Glenloan on the West coast, a terrace of cottages. For the first time in my life I didn't have to work. And I thought, why should I put up with the adolescent vagaries of inky boys when I much prefer books?'

'And inky boys presumably don't appreciate books?'

'No. Some seemed to—appeared to be interested, but...' He rose abruptly. 'A bite to eat perhaps?'

Half a Stilton and Bath Olivers were produced. The evening passed pleasantly. They munched and drank, swapped quotations and examined the books. Their crossword minds clicked, and allusion and anecdote circled round each other. It was the sort of mild intellectual exercise that Charles had not indulged in since his undergraduate days. Very pleasant, floating on a cloud of malt whisky above everyday life. The book-lined room promised to be a welcome sanctuary from the earnest denim below.

Eventually Charles looked at his watch. Nearly one o'clock. 'I must go down to the bear-pit.'

'Don't bother. I'll make up the sofa for you here.'

'No, no. Downstairs is the bed I have chosen, and I must lie on it.'

The bed he had chosen had been left vacant for good

reason. At half-past three he woke to discover it had come adrift in the middle and was trying to fold him up like a book. He wrestled with it in the sweaty breathing dorm and then tottered along to the lavatory.

It was locked and a strange sound came from inside. As Charles took advantage of the washbasin in the adjacent bathroom, he identified the noise through a haze of malt. It was a man crying.

CHAPTER TWO

The very sky turns pale above;
   The earth grows dark beneath;
The human Terror thrills with cold,
   And draws a shorter breath—
An universal panic owns
   The dread approach of DEATH!

              THE ELM TREE

THE EDINBURGH FREEMASONS' revenue must shoot up during the Festival, because they seem to own practically every strange little hall in the city. Each year the gilded columns of these painted rooms witness the latest excesses of Fringe drama, and the gold-leaf names of Grand Masters gaze unmoved at satire, light-shows, nudity or God-rock, according to theatrical fashion.

On the Monday morning the Temple of the Masonic Hall, Lauriston Place, was undergoing *A Midsummer Night's Dream*, Shakespeare's Immortal Comedy Revisualised by Stella Galpin-Lord. As Charles Paris slipped in, it was clear that the process of revisualisation had hit a snag. The snag was that Stella Galpin-Lord was having a directorial tantrum.

'Where are those bloody fairies? Didn't you hear your bloody cue? For Christ's sake, concentrate! Bottom, get up off your backside . . .'

As she fulminated, it was clear to Charles that Stella Galpin-Lord was not a student. Far from it. The over-dramatic name fitted the over-dramatic figure. She was wearing rehearsal black, a polo-necked pullover tight over her presentable bosom, and clinging flared trousers less kind to her less presentable bottom. Honey-blonded hair was scraped back into a broad knotted scarf. The efforts of make-up—skilful pancake, elaborate eyes and a hard line of lipstick—drew attention to what they aimed to disguise. The slack skin of her face gave the impression of a badly erected tent, here and there pulled tight by misplaced guy-ropes. The tantrum and her twitchy manner with a cigarette spelt trouble to Charles. Neurotic middle-aged actresses are a hazard of the profession.

'Well, don't just amble on. You're meant to be fairies, not navvies. For God's sake! Amateurs! This show opens in less than a week and we don't get in the hall again till Thursday. Good God, if you don't know the lines now . . . Where is the prompter? Where is the bloody prompter!'

Charles, who had only come down to check the details of staging in the hall, decided it could wait and sidled out.

Back in Coates Gardens he looked for somewhere to work. In the men's dormitory a youth was strumming a guitar with all the versatility of a metronome. Sounds from upstairs indicated a revue rehearsal in the girls' room. Charles felt tempted to seek sanctuary with James Milne again, but decided it might be an imposition. He went down to the dining-room. Mercifully it was empty.

With a tattered script of *So Much Comic, So Much Blood* open on the table, he started thumbing through an ancient copy of Jerrold's edition of Hood, looking for *The Dundee Guide*, an early poem which might add a little local interest for an Edinburgh audience. It was not there. He was perplexed for a moment, until he remembered that only a fragment of the work survived and was in the *Memorials of Thomas Hood*. He started thumbing through that.

So Much Comic, So Much Blood had begun life as a half-hour radio programme. Then Charles had added to the compilation and done the show for a British Council audience. Over the years he had inserted different poems, played up the comic element and dramatised some of the letters. The result was a good hour's show and he was proud of it.

He was also proud that its evolution predated the success of Roy Dotrice in John Aubrey's *Brief Lives*, which had set every actor in the country ransacking literary history for one-man shows.

'I'm going to make some coffee. Would you like some?' Charles looked up at the girl in the photograph, Anna Duncan.

'Please.' She disappeared into the kitchen. He stared with less interest at the extant fragments of *The Dundee Guide*.

'Here's the coffee. Do carry on.'

'Don't worry. I like being disturbed. I'm Charles Paris.'

'I know. Recognise you from the box. It's very good of you to step into the breach.'

'I gather you did more or less the same thing.'

'Yes. Poor Lesley.' A brief pause. 'What is your show about?'

'Thomas Hood.'

She did not recognise the name. 'Why's it called what it is?'

'Because he once wrote "No gentleman alive has written so much Comic and spitten so much blood within six consecutive years". In a letter to *The Athenaeum* actually.'

'Oh. I don't think I've even heard of Thomas Hood.'

'I'm sure you know his poems.'

'Do I?'

'Yes. "I remember, I remember..."'

' "... the house where I was born"? That one? I didn't know that was Hood.'

'It was. And *No-vember*. *Faithless Sally Brown*. Lots of stuff.'

'Oh.'

Her eyes were unusual. Very dark, almost navy blue. Her bare arm on the table was sunburned, its haze of tiny hairs bleached golden.

'What are you reading at Derby?'

'French and Drama in theory. Drama in practice.'

'Last year?'

'One more. If I bother.' The navy eyes stared at him evenly. It was pleasantly disconcerting.

'I've just been down to the hall. Saw the lovely Stella Galpin-Lord. A mature student, I thought.'

Anna laughed. 'She lectures in Drama.'

'Ah. She seemed rather to have lost her temper this morning.'

'That's unusual. She's always uptight, but doesn't often actually explode.'

'She was exploding this morning.'

'Everyone's getting on each other's nerves. Living like sardines in this place. I'm glad I'm in a flat up here.' (On reflection, Charles was glad she was too.) 'And people keep arguing about who's rehearsing what when, and who's in the hall. It's purgatory.'

'You're rehearsing the revue at the moment?'

'Yes, but I've got a break. They're doing a new number— about Nixon's resignation and Ford coming in. Trying to be topical.'

'Is the revue going to be good?'

'Bits.'

'Bits?' Charles smiled. Anna smiled back.

At that moment Pam Northcliffe bounced into the room, her arms clutching two carrier bags which she spilled out on the table. 'Hello. Oh Lord, I must write my expenses. I'm spending so much on props.'

'What have you been buying?' asked Charles.

'Oh Lord, lots of stuff for *Mary*.'

'Did you get the cardboard for my ruff?'

'No, Anna, will do, promise. No, I was getting black crepe for the execution. And all these knives that I've got to make retractable. And some make-up and stuff.'

'Good old Leichner's,' said Charles, picking up a bottle which had rolled out of one of the carriers. It was labelled 'Arterial Blood'.

'What other sort is there?'

'There's a brighter one, for surface cuts. It's called . . .'

Pam paused for a moment. '. . . oh, I forget.' And she bustled on. 'Look, I'm not going to be in your way, am I? I've got to do these knives. I was going to do them on the table, if you . . .'

'No, it's O.K. I've finished.' Charles resigned himself to the inevitable. Anna returned to her rehearsal and he went to see if the men's dormitory was still being serenaded.

Passing the office, he heard sounds of argument, Michael Vanderzee's voice, more Dutch in anger, struggling against Brian Cassells' diplomatic tones. '. . . and the whole rehearsal was ruined yesterday because that bloody fool Willy wasn't there. Look, I need more time in the hall.'

'So does everyone.'

'But I've lost a day.'

'That's not my fault, Mike. Look, I've worked out a schedule that's fair to everyone.'

'Bugger your schedule.'

'It's there on the wall-chart—'

'Oh, bugger your wall-chart!' Michael Vanderzee flung himself out of the office, past Charles, to the front door. The windows shook as it slammed behind him.

Brian Cassells appeared in the hall looking flushed. When he saw Charles, he smoothed down his pin-striped suit as if nothing had happened. 'Ah, morning.' The efficient young executive was reborn. 'I've . . . er . . . I've got your posters. Just picked them up.'

'Oh, great.'

'In the office.'

On the desk were two rectangular brown paper parcels. 'A thousand in each,' said Brian smugly. 'Did the Letrasetting myself. Do have a look.'

Charles tore the paper and slid one of the printed sheets out. As he looked at it, Brian Cassells grinned. 'O.K.?'

Charles passed the paper over. It was headed :

D.U.D.S. ON THE FRINGE
. . . and the greatest of these is Charles Paris' *So Much Comic, So Much Blood.*

23

'Oh,' said Brian, 'I am sorry.'

Undisturbed rehearsal in the Coates Gardens house was clearly impossible. Charles decided a jaunt to one of his Edinburgh favourites, the Museum of Childhood in the Royal Mile, might not come amiss. It was only Monday and there was a whole week till he had to face an audience. And with Brian Cassells in charge of publicity, the chances were against there being an audience anyway.

Back at the house late afternoon, he found Martin Warburton hovering in the hall, as if waiting for him. 'You're Charles Paris, aren't you?'

'Yes.'

'I've written this play. *Who Now?* We're doing it. I want you to read it.' A fifth carbon copy was thrust forward.

'Oh, thank you. I'd like to.'

'You don't know. You might like to; you might think it was a waste of time.'

'I'm sure you wouldn't have written it if you thought it was a waste of time.'

The boy looked at Charles fiercely for a moment, then burst into loud laughter. 'Yes, I might. That's exactly what I might have done.'

'Why?'

'Everything we do is just random. I happened to write this. It's just chance. I might have written anything else. It's nothing.'

'I know sometimes it seems like that, but very few things are random—'

'Don't patronise me!' Martin's shout was suddenly loud, as if the volume control on his voice had broken. He reached out to snatch the play back, then changed his mind, rushed out of the house and slammed the door.

In spite of Brian Cassells' assurances, the Masonic Hall was not free for Charles to rehearse in on the Tuesday afternoon. When he arrived at two o'clock Michael Vanderzee

24

had just started a workshop session with the *Mary* cast and most of the *Dream* lot too. Brian was not there to appeal to (he'd apparently gone down to London for a Civil Service interview), so Charles sat at the back of the hall and waited.

Everyone except Michael was lying stretched out on the floor. '... and relax. Feel each part of your body go. From the extremities. Right, your fingers and toes, now your hands and feet. Now the forearms and your calves—feel them go ...'

Charles' attitude to this sort of theatre was ambivalent. He had no objection to movement classes and workshop techniques. They were useful exercises for actors, and kept them from getting over-analytical about their 'art'. All good stuff. Until there was a show to put on. At that point they became irrelevant and the expediency of getting everything ready for the opening left no time for self-indulgence.

Michael Vanderzee (who drew inspiration from the physical disciplines of East and West and created a theatre indissolubly integrated with working life) obviously did not share these views. 'Right. O.K. Now I want you to sit in pairs, and when I clap, you start to tell each other fairy stories. And you've got to concentrate so hard, you tell your story and you don't listen to the other guy. Really concentrate. O.K. I clap my hands.'

While the assembly shouted out a cacophony of Red Riding Hood and Goldilocks, Charles looked down at Anna. Squatting on the floor, mouthing nonsense, she still appeared supremely self-possessed. Her T-shirt did nothing to hide her contours and the interest she had started in him was strengthened.

The door of the hall opened noisily. An enormously tall young man in blue denim with a Jesus Christ hairstyle strolled purposefully up the aisle. 'Willy!' roared Michael. 'Where the hell have you been? Why weren't you at rehearsal this morning?'

'I had things to do.' The voice was sharp and the accent Scottish.

'You've got things to do here as well. I had to drag you in yesterday.'

'Piss off.' Willy collapsed into a chair in the front row, ungainly as a stick insect.

'Look, do you want to be in this show or not? You've got to rehearse.'

'I don't mind rehearsing, but I don't see why I should waste time poncing about with relaxation and pretending I'm a pineapple and all that. I'm only meant to be doing the music.'

'You're playing Rizzio in the show, and you're meant to be part of an ensemble.'

Willy gave a peculiarly Scottish dismissive snort. 'All right, all right. What do you want me to do?'

'I want you to shout, all of you. Scream your heads off. Really uninhibited screams. Let everything go. Right. When I clap.'

The noise was appalling. Charles sunk into his chair with hands over his ears. It was going to be a long time before he got the stage to himself.

When the baying mouths onstage had finally closed, he uncovered his ears and heard another sound close behind him. A sniff. He turned to see the ship-wrecked face of Stella Galpin-Lord, who had just slipped into the hall. She saw him and blew her nose.

At that moment Pam Northcliffe bustled in, her arms as ever full of parcels and packages. 'Hello, Charles,' she hissed loudly. He grinned at her.

'Just brought down the props for the *Mary* photo-call.'

'All O.K.?' he whispered.

'Oh Lord, I suppose so. Just about. I was up till two last night doing the daggers.'

'Work all right?'

'Yes.' She showed him her artefacts proudly. Charles picked up one of the knives. Its metal blade had been replaced by silver-painted plastic which slid neatly back into the handle. He pressed it into his hand. 'Very good.'

'Oh. I'm afraid the paint's not quite dry.'

Charles looked down at the silver smudge on his palm. 'Never mind.'

'What's Mike up to now?'

'God knows.'

'All right. Now we're relaxed, all uninhibited. Now an ensemble is people who know each other. Love each other, hate each other. We try hate. Right, as we've done it before. Somebody stands in the middle and the others shout hatred at him. Doesn't matter what you say, any lies, anything. Hate, hate. We purge the emotions.

'O.K., Willy, you first. Stand in the middle. We form a circle round. And we shout. Ah, hello, Stella, you join our workshop?'

'Might learn something,' she said patronisingly.

'You might, you might. Hey, Charles Paris. You want to learn something too?'

Charles choked back his first instinctive rejoinder and meekly said, 'Yes, O.K.' Enter into the spirit of the thing. Don't be a middle-aged fuddy-duddy.

The large circle around Willy Mariello waited for the signal. Michael clapped his hands and they shouted. Abuse poured out. Young faces swelled with obscenities. Stella Galpin-Lord screamed, 'Bastard! Bastard!' her mouth twisting and pulling a whole map of new lines on her face. Anna's expression was cold and white. Martin Warburton almost gibbered with excitement. And Charles himself found it distressingly easy to succumb, to scream with them. It was frightening.

Another clap. They subsided, panting. 'Good. Catharsis. Good. O.K. Now someone else. Charles.'

It was not pleasant. As the mob howled, he concentrated on Sydney Carton, borne on his tumbril to the scaffold. 'It is a far, far better thing that I do now . . .' It still was not pleasant.

But a clap ended it and another victim was chosen. Then another and another. The repetition took the edge off the discomfort of being abused. Just an exercise. They finished, breathless.

'O.K. Another concentration exercise. Truth Game. You sit on the ground in pairs and ask each other questions. You have to answer with the truth instantly. If you hesitate, you start asking the questions. And don't cheat. It's more difficult than you think.'

They started forming pairs. Charles saw Willy Mariello speak to Anna. She turned away and sat down opposite a colourless girl in faded denim. Willy and Charles were the only ones left standing. They squatted opposite each other.

The Scotsman sat awkwardly, his long legs bent under him like pipe-cleaners. Stuck to his denim shirt was a purple badge with white lettering: *It's Scotland's Oil.* The long messianic hair was full of white powder and the hands were flecked with white paint. His expression was aggressive and he had the hard mouth of a spoilt child. But the brown eyes were troubled.

Charles tried to think of something to ask. 'What do you make of all these exercises?'

'I think they're a bloody waste of time.' The answer was instant, no question about the truth there. Voices started up around and made concentration difficult.

'Um. Are you happy?'

'No.'

'Why not?'

'A lot of hassles.'

'Anything specific?'

'Yes.'

The concentration of talking and listening over the other voices was intense. Everything seemed focused in this one conversation. Charles pressed further. 'What's worrying you?'

Willy hesitated. Then, 'I've found out something I'd rather not know, something that might be dangerous.'

'Something about a person?'

'Yes.'

'Someone connected with this group?'

28

A slight pause. 'Yes.' There was fear in the brown eyes. Charles pushed on, mesmerised by the direction of the conversation. 'Who?'

Willy opened his mouth, but paused for a moment. Stella Galpin-Lord's piercing voice was suddenly isolated. '. . . and lost my virginity when I was fourteen . . .' The spell was broken. 'No, I didn't come in quick enough,' said Willy. 'I ask. How old are you?'

The exercise continued, but Charles felt a vague unease.

The Truth Game was followed by a Contact Game. 'O.K.? We close our eyes and move around. When you touch somebody, you make contact. Feel, explore, encounter. Get to know them with your hands. This will increase your perceptions. O.K.?'

Perhaps it was by chance that the first person Charles touched was Anna. In accord with his director's instructions, he made contact, felt, explored, encountered and got to know her with his hands. Her eyes opened to a slit of navy blue. He smiled. She smiled.

'Are you rehearsing tonight?'

'No.'

'Fancy dinner?'

'O.K.'

Charles moved away to feel, explore and encounter someone else. His probing hand felt the arm of a tweed jacket, then up, over a chest criss-crossed with leather straps to the bristly wool of a beard.

'What the hell do you think you're doin'?' The voice had the broken-bottle edge of Glasgow in it. 'I'm the photographer. Who's Michael Vanderzee?'

Getting people into costume took some time. The photographer fretted and cursed. Then Michael announced he did not want posed shots; he wanted natural action shots. That involved rehearsing whole chunks of the play. The photographer cursed more.

'Right, come on. Let's do the scene of Rizzio's murder.

O.K.? You'll get some good shots from this. Action stuff. Violence.'

'How long's the bloody scene?'

'We'll only do the end. Three, four minutes.'

'Why you can't just pose them ... I've got some fashion pictures to do later this afternoon.'

'I don't want them to look like amateur theatricals.'

'Why not? That's what they bloody are.'

The scene started and Charles sat under a light at the back of the hall to watch. *Mary, Queen of Sots* was written in a blank verse that was meant to sound archaic but only sounded twee. Since Willy needed a prompt every other line, it was heavy going.

'Willy, for God's sake!'

'Shut up, Michael!' The tall figure looked incongruous in doublet and hose.

'Look, for Christ's sake, can't we get these bloody photos taken? My time's expensive and these models are waiting.'

'I say, we haven't got the daggers,' said Martin Warburton suddenly from the recesses of a dramatic conspirator's cloak.

'Oh, Pam, where the hell are they? Here, quick. Look, the blades retract on the spring like this. O.K.? Now come on, let's get it right first time.' Charles started to scan his *So Much Comic* ... script.

Suddenly his eyes were jerked off the page by a scream. Not a theatrical workshop scream, but an authentic spine-tingling cry of horror from Stella Galpin-Lord.

Onstage the scene was frozen. Anna stood white-faced in her black Tudor costume, looking down at Willy Mariello, whose great length had shrunk into a little heap on the stage. Around him were a circle of cloaked conspirators clutching daggers with retracted blades. In the centre Martin Warburton gazed fascinated at the weapon in his hand. Its blade was metal and the Arterial Blood which dripped from it was not made by Leichner's.

CHAPTER THREE

The BLOODY HAND significant of crime,
That glaring on the old heraldic banner,
Had kept its crimson unimpaired by time,
In such a wondrous manner.

THE HAUNTED HOUSE

THE POLICE ARRIVED promptly and were very efficient. An ambulance took Willy to hospital, but he was dead on arrival. Everyone gave statements and was told to expect further enquiries. Pam Northcliffe and Martin Warburton were taken away for extended questioning. A distraught Pam was returned to Coates Gardens in the early hours of the Wednesday morning and treated in the girls' dormitory with sleeping-pills and inquisitive sympathy.

The atmosphere in the house throughout the Wednesday was charged with tension. The accumulated pressures of living together and building up to the shows' openings were aggravated by the shock of Willy's death. Rehearsal schedules were thrown out and the continual reappearance of policemen at the house and hall got on everyone's nerves. All day Coates Gardens was full of uneasy jokes, sudden flares of temper and bursts of weeping.

Charles escaped the worst of it. Fortunately James Milne had suggested that he might be glad of a little seclusion from the community hysterics and offered the sanctuary of his flat. It was a great relief to be with someone who did not want to discuss the death. Milne dismissed the subject. 'I didn't know the boy well and I wasn't there at the time, so I don't feel too involved. It's an unpleasant business. And the best thing to do about unpleasant things is to put them out of your mind.'

But Charles did not find it so easy. He felt he was involved and, as he tried to concentrate on revising *So Much Comic ...*, his mind kept returning to the scene in the Masonic Hall. He suffered from the communal shock. And another uncomfortable feeling which he did not want to investigate.

By the Thursday morning the atmosphere among the D.U.D.S. was more settled. The Procurator-Fiscal's enquiry (which is held instead of a public inquest in Scotland) was no doubt following its private course, but the students were unaffected by it. Only Martin Warburton remained hysterical, which was hardly surprising after his long ordeal of questioning.

The police were not making any charges against him and, though the investigation was far from complete, the general impression was that they considered the death to have been a ghastly accident. The real knife had been put in one of Pam's carrier bags with the treated ones by mistake and foul play was apparently not suspected.

On the Thursday afternoon rehearsals restarted in earnest. More than in earnest, in panic. Everyone realised at the same time that a day and a half had been lost and there were still three shows opening on the following Monday. Brian Cassells' rehearsal schedule was ignored. (Since its originator was still in London he could not argue.) Stella Galpin-Lord commandeered the Masonic Hall for the rest of the day as her right and Michael Vanderzee demanded it for the Friday. Charles began to think he would be lucky to get onstage there for his actual performances. Rehearsal in the house was equally impossible. In the basement Pam and a couple of A.S.M.s were building a wall for Pyramus and Thisbe. Three smelly technicians lay over a greasy lighting plot in the men's dormitory. The Laird's flat was locked and silent. In fact Charles was relieved; his mind was too full for serious rehearsal.

Still, as a gesture of good faith, he tucked his script and Hood's *Collected Poems* under his arm before he set off into the city. It was a warm afternoon and only five o'clock. There were lots of places to sit and study in Edinburgh— Princes Street Gardens, the Castle, or it might even be worth a stroll down to Arthur's Seat. He weighed the possibilities, but was not surprised when he went straight into the nearest pub and ordered a large whisky.

He sat hunched at the bar and realised that he could not put off thinking any longer. And the one thought which he had been holding back for nearly two days resolved itself clearly in his mind.

Whatever the police thought, Willy Mariello had been murdered.

Charles could not forget the expression in those brown eyes during the Truth Game, when Willy had spoken of finding out something about someone that he would rather not know. There had been pain in that look, but also there had been fear, even horror. Whatever it was that he had found out it was nasty. Nasty enough for someone to commit murder to keep it quiet.

Charles had tried to express this suspicion to the detective who took his statement, but he knew the man did not take it seriously. Somehow the words had not come out right. 'It was a moment of such concentration . . . I could see such fear in his eyes . . . It made me feel a sense of danger . . .' The further he got into it, the more tenuous the idea seemed and the more Charles knew he sounded like an effete actor emoting. In spite of polite assurances about complete investigations, that was obviously what the detective took him for. By the time he got to Charles, he had probably had a bellyful of the 'vague feelings' and 'premonitions' of self-dramatising students.

And, objectively, it did sound pretty nonsensical. Charles, whose normal thought processes involved reducing everything he did to the absurd and seeing if there was anything left, was surprised that the conviction remained so strong. But it did. It was an instinct he could not deny.

Facing the fact that Willy had been murdered led

automatically to the question of what should be done about it. Charles had done his duty as a citizen by voicing his suspicions, and it was quite possible that the police were already way ahead of him, working on investigations of their own. He was no longer involved.

But involvement does not cease like that. It was easy enough for James Milne to say he wanted to forget about it; he had not sat opposite Willy in the Truth Game, he had not been present at the killing.

Charles knew he had to get to the bottom of it. He recalled an earlier occasion when he had come up against crime, in the case of Marius Steen. Then he had been forced into involvement by circumstance; this time he was making a positive decision. He was not driven by any crusading fervour for the cause of justice, but he knew he would not feel at peace until he had found out all the facts.

And the only facts he had were that Willy Mariello had found out something unpleasant about one of the people involved with the Derby University Dramatic Society in Edinburgh. And that he had subsequently been killed by a dagger in the hand of Martin Warburton.

No more facts. Now on to feelings. Charles had a strong feeling that the one person who did not kill Willy was Martin Warburton. Unless he were a lunatic or playing some incredibly devious game of his own, no one would commit a premeditated murder in front of thirty people, under stage lights, with a photographer on hand. And unless Charles' suspicions about the motive were wrong, the murder was premeditated.

The elimination of Martin still left about forty suspects. Any of the students themselves or of the hangers-on who surrounded the D.U.D.S. could have switched one of the treated knives for a real one, and so stood a reasonable, though not infallible, chance of killing Willy Mariello.

Charles ordered another large whisky. A little mild investigation was called for.

*   *   *

34

Things could not have worked out better when he returned to Coates Gardens. Pam Northcliffe was in the dining-room alone mixing porridge to roughcast Pyramus and Thisbe's wall. The cooks of the day were clattering about in the kitchen preparing a dinner whose main ingredient smelled like cabbage.

Pam looked up, red-eyed and guilty when he entered. 'Hello.'

'Hi. Feeling better?'

'Yes.' Spoken with determination.

'I was going down to the pub for a drink and looking for someone to join me. Do you fancy it?'

'What? Me?'

'Yes.'

'Well, I . . .' She wiped a porridgy hand on the back of her jeans, adding another streak to the existing collage. 'All right.'

A half of lager for Pam and, since he was now thirsty, a pint of 'heavy' for Charles. 'How are the props? Coming together?'

'I think so. I'm spending over my budget on them.'

'D.U.D.S. will find the money.'

'I hope so.' She spoke with great care, as if the accumulated tension inside her might break out at the slightest provocation.

Charles knew that discussion of Willy's death might be exactly that sort of provocation. But it was what he had to investigate. He approached obliquely. 'Everyone settling down a bit now.'

'Yes, I suppose so. All too busy to think about it.'

'That's a blessing.'

'Yes.' Silence. Charles tried to think how he could get her back on to the subject without causing too much pain. But fortunately he did not have to. She seemed anxious to talk it out of her system without prompting. 'I don't think I'll ever get over it. It's the first time I've ever seen someone dead.'

35

'It is nasty. But you do forget.'

'I mean, you see it on films, and on the box and it all . . . well, it doesn't seem important. But when you actually see . . .' Her lower lip started to quiver.

'Don't talk about it.'

As Charles hoped, she ignored his advice. 'And the trouble is . . . apart from just the shock and things, I feel responsible. I mean, I was in charge of the props, so I must have got the knives mixed up.'

'Do you really think you did?'

'Oh Lord, I just don't know now. I would have said definitely not. I remember counting them before I put them in my carrier bag. The police asked me all this and, you know, at the end I couldn't remember what I'd done. You think so much about something, after a time you just don't know what's true any more . . .'

'I know what you mean.'

'And it's so stupid, because I shouldn't have done the knives like that anyway. Michael Vanderzee told me what he wanted, and I thought the best thing would be to get real knives with hollow handles and unscrew them and take the blades out. And Michael said that was daft and expensive and I should have improvised and . . .' Her voice wavered with the remembered rebuke. 'It's the first time I've done props. And I got it all wrong. If I hadn't done the knives that way, Willy would still be alive.'

Charles did not feel so certain of that. He felt sure that if the knives had not been to hand, the murderer would have found some other method. But it was not the moment to voice such suspicions. 'Pam, you really mustn't blame yourself. Even if you did mix the knives up. And it's quite possible that you didn't. Somebody else may have been playing about with them and made the mistake. I mean, presumably they were just lying round the house, so anyone could get at them?' He left the question hanging disingenuously in the air.

'Yes. I suppose so.'

36

'Toy knives have a fascination for people. Anyone might have started fooling around with them. How long were they there?'

'I was up late finishing them on Monday night. And I left them out on the table till the next morning.'

'Why? So that the paint could dry?'

'Yes, but it didn't actually. I got some awful oily lacquer that stayed sticky for ages.'

'Was the real knife with the others?'

'Yes, it was. You see, it was daft, but I was sort of rather proud of the ones I'd made because they did look so realistic. So I left them all out on the table.'

'So that people would see them when they came down to breakfast?'

'Yes.' She looked sheepish. 'I haven't made lots of things and I thought they looked good.'

'They did. Look very good.' He almost added 'Unfortunately', but realised that might be tactless. 'So then they were put away while people had breakfast?'

'Yes, I put them in a carrier bag, and I thought I left the real one in a box with my scissors and sellotape and glue and all that rubbish.'

'And they stayed in your carrier bag in the sitting-room till you brought them down to the hall at about three o'clock?'

'Yes.'

'So there was lots of time for anyone in the house to play around with them during the day and mix them up?'

'I suppose so.'

'You weren't there during the morning?'

'No, I had to go out to buy some cardboard and stuff.'

'Well, I should think that's what happened. Someone was fooling about with them on the Tuesday morning and mixed them up.' It was not what he really meant, but Pam looked reassured. What he did mean was that the knives had been on show for every member of the company, that the murderer had realised their potential and arranged the switch when the sitting-room was empty at some point during the Tuesday morning. Then he had had to wait and see what happened. Which might well have been nothing. The chances were that someone would notice the real knife before the stabbing could take place, and the murderer would have to find another method. But the impatience of the photographer at the photo-call had given no one time to inspect their weapons closely.

Though the murder method was now clear, the identity of its deviser remained obscure. From Pam's account, virtually anyone who was in the house on the Tuesday morning could have switched the knives. And that meant virtually every member of the D.U.D.S. company. Which in turn meant checking everyone's movements. Which sounded a long, boring process.

'Did you know Willy Mariello well?' Charles tried another tack.

Pam blushed. 'No, hardly at all.'

'But you must have seen him round the University.'

'What do you mean?'

'During term-time. If he was involved in the Dramatic Society.'

'Oh, but he wasn't. He was nothing to do with the University.'

'Then where did he come from?'

'He used to play with Puce.'

'What?'

'The rock band. He was lead guitar. Until they broke up earlier this year. Oh, come on, you've heard of Puce.'

Charles had to confess he hadn't.

They walked back to Coates Gardens together. Pam seemed calmer; she had almost recaptured her customary bounce. A nice girl. No beauty, but good-natured. Needed a man who appreciated her.

She was telling him about her parents' home in Somerset as they entered the hall. At that moment Anna Duncan came out of the Office. 'Hello,' said Charles. She grinned.

Pam paused in mid-sentence: He realised his rudeness. 'I'm so sorry. I . . . what were you saying?'

'Oh, it wasn't important. I'd better get on with my wall.' And she disappeared gracelessly downstairs.

'Taking other women out when you've already stood me up,' said Anna with mock reproach.

'I hardly think we'd have had a very relaxed dinner with policemen taking statements between courses.'

'No, I didn't mean it.'

'Rehearsing tonight?'

'Finishing at half past eight.'

'Shall we pretend the last two days haven't happened, and pick up where we left off?'

'That sounds a nice idea.'

'Shall I see you here?'

'No. If Mike gives us another of his rolling about on the floor workshops, I'll need to go back to the flat and have a quick bath.'

'Well, let's meet at the restaurant. Do you know L'Etoile?'

'In Grindlay Street?'

'That's the one. I'll book a table for half past nine. O.K.?'

'Fine. I must get back upstairs and pretend to be a banana.'

'Another of Michael Vanderzee's wonderful ideas?'

'Yes. The perception through inanimate transference of pure emotion.'

'Wow.'

Anna grinned again and left. Charles knocked on the office door. If Brian was back, perhaps it would be possible to arrange some rehearsal time at the Masonic Hall.

The Company Manager was wearing another executive suit, this time a beige three-piece. Charles explained his requirements and was not wholly reassured by Brian's assurance that he'd sort it out and the movement of some coloured strips on the wall-chart. There are certain sorts of efficiency which do not inspire confidence.

The efficiency had obviously been at work on the 'What

the Press says about D.U.D.S.' board. It was smothered with cuttings about the death of Willy Mariello. The one person to have made a definite profit from the killing was the disgruntled Glaswegian photographer. He seemed to have sold the pictures to every newspaper in the country. Charles felt a frisson of shock at seeing the scene again. 'You're not actually going to use those as publicity?'

'No,' said Brian regretfully, 'wouldn't be quite the thing. Not to display them. Mind you, it is an amazing spread. It's really fixed the name of D.U.D.S. in people's minds. Better than any publicity stunt you could devise. I remember last year Cambridge staged something about pretending Elizabeth Taylor was in Edinburgh. They got a girl to dress up as her and so on. Quite a lot of coverage. But nothing like this.'

The note of unashamed satisfaction in Brian's voice made Charles look at him curiously. Insensitivity of that order would be wasted in the Civil Service; he should try for advertising or television. 'I'm sure Willy would be glad to think that his life was lost in the cause of full houses for the D.U.D.S.'

'Yes, it's an ill wind.' Brian was impervious to irony.

'One thing . . . I was interested to hear that Willy Mariello wasn't a member of the University.'

'No.'

'How did he come to be involved in this then?'

'I don't know. I suppose he was a friend of someone.'

'Who? Do you know?'

'No. I don't know any of them very well. I wasn't in D.U.D.S. I was Chairman of Ducker.'

'Ducker?'

'D.U.C.A. Derby University Conservative Association.'

'Oh.'

'They only brought me into this because of my administrative ability.'

The men's dormitory was mercifully empty and Charles managed an undisturbed run of *So Much Comic, So Much*

Blood. He was encouraged to find how much he remembered. The intonation of the poems came back naturally and he began to feel the rhythm of the whole show. A bit more work and it could be quite good.

So he felt confident as he sat opposite Anna in the French restaurant in Grindlay Street. Her appearance contributed to his mood. The 'quick bath' back at her flat had included a flattering amount of preparation. Just-pressed pale yellow shirt with a silly design of foxtrotting dancers on it, beautifully cut black velvet trousers. Eyelashes touched with mascara, lip-coloured lipstick, cropped hair flopping with controlled abandon. All very casual, but carefully done.

'I'm looking forward to seeing the show. I'm sorry, as I said, I don't know anything about Hood.'

'Not many people do.'

'Was he Scottish?'

'No. His father came from Dundee, but Thomas himself only went there a couple of times. Wasn't very struck with it either. Particularly the cooking. "I sicken with disgust at sight of a singed sheep's head. I cannot bring myself to endure oatmeal, which I think harsh, dry and insipid. The only time I ever took it with any kind of relish was one day on a trouting party, when I was hungry enough to eat anything." Sorry, I've just been working on it, hence the long trailer.'

'What do you do in the show—dress up as Hood?'

'No, it wouldn't work. I don't like all that emotive bit—this is what the bloke was *really like*. It seems to remove the subject from reality rather than making him more real. Like historical novels about Famous People. I'm just an interpreter of Hood's work; I don't pretend to be him. Let the poems and lyrics speak for themselves. Certainly in the case of the poems, it would falsify them to read them in character. They were written as public entertainments to be recited and that's how I treat them.'

'So it's more a sort of recital than an acting thing?'

'I suppose so. It's mid-way between. And it has the great

advantage that I don't have to learn it all and can actually refer to the book when I want to.'

'Handy. So you just wear ordinary clothes for it?'

'A suit, maybe. I'd look daft dressed as Thomas Hood anyway. I haven't the figure of a stunted Victorian consumptive.'

'He was another one, was he?'

'Yes. Hence the *So Much Blood* of the title. Actually there is some question as to whether it was consumption—T.B. or not T.B. It may have been rheumatic heart disease. But he spat blood, that's the main thing. It was very difficult to be a literary figure in Victorian times without spitting blood. Healthy writers started at an enormous disadvantage.'

Anna laughed. 'If he was ill, I think you're showing great restraint in not acting it out. Most actors leap at the chance of doing hacking coughs and their dramatic dying bit.'

'So do I. But unfortunately it wouldn't be right for this show. Oh, I've died with the best of them. You should have heard my death rattle as Richard II after Sir Pierce of Exton stabbed me.'

There was a moment's pause. They were both thinking the same, both seeing Willy Mariello lying on the stage at the Masonic Hall. Anna went pale.

'Sorry. Shouldn't have said that. I wasn't thinking.'

'It's all right. It's just . . . so recent.'

'Yes.' Charles hesitated. He had decided to investigate Willy's death, but dinner with Anna was not intended to be part of that investigation; her attraction for him was not primarily as a source of information. On the other hand, here was someone who knew all the people involved, and the conversation had come round to the subject. The detective instinct overcame his baser ones. 'Did you know Willy well?'

'No, I wouldn't say well. I knew him.'

'I was amazed to discover that he wasn't at the University. How on earth did he get involved with your lot?'

'Oh, he . . . You know he used to play with a band?'

'Yes. Puce.'

'That's right. They came and did a gig at our Student's Union. I think Willy stayed around a bit. It was just round the period the band broke up. He must have met the drama lot then.'

'And somebody asked him to do this show?'

'I suppose so, yes. Because he lived in Edinburgh and was kind of at a loose end. He wrote all the music, you see. I think he wanted to do something different, after the band.'

'*Mary, Queen of Sots* sounds pretty different. You don't know if he made any particular friends at Derby?'

'No.' She seemed to remember something. 'Oh, yes. Sam. Sam Wasserman. He's the guy who wrote *Mary*. I think Willy was friendly with him. Probably it was Sam who asked him to do the music.'

'I don't think I've met Sam.'

'No. He's not up here. On holiday in Europe somewhere. He's American so it has to be Europe rather than any specific country. They seem to think Europe is just one country.'

'So Sam's not likely to be up here at all?'

'I think he's coming up for the opening of *Mary*.'

'When's that?'

'Third week. Opens on the 2nd September.'

'Ah.' A week after Charles' engagement finished. No chance of picking Sam Wasserman's brains. The investigation did not seem to be proceeding very fast. He decided that he would forget it for the rest of the evening. 'How's your show going?'

'*Mary*'s still all over the place. We spend so much time improvising and so on, we hardly ever get near the actual script.'

'And the revue?'

'Still bits. Bits are O.K. One or two of the songs are quite exciting, but . . . I don't know. See what the audience thinks on the first night.'

'Monday. I'll be there. Hmm. I wonder what I should call my opening. A first lunch?'

'Why not? I'll come and see it, rehearsals permitting.'

43

'Good.' Charles refilled her glass from the cold bottle of Vouvray. 'Do you want to make the theatre your career?'

'Yes.' No hesitation. 'Always have. Totally stage-struck.'

'Hmm.'

'There was a world of cynicism in that grunt. You, I take it, are not stage-struck?'

'More stage-battered at my age.'

'Don't you still find it exciting?'

'Not very often, no. I can't really imagine doing anything else, but as a profession it leaves a lot to be desired. Like money, security . . .'

'I know.'

'There's a lot more to it than talent. You need lots of help. You have to be tough and calculating.'

'I know.'

'I'm sorry. I sound awfully middle-aged. I think the prime reason for that is that I am awfully middle-aged. No, it's just that I'd hate to think of anyone going into the business who didn't know what it was about.'

'I do know.'

'Yes. So you're prepared for all that unemployment they talk about, sitting by the telephone, sleeping with fat old directors.'

'I only sleep with who I want to sleep with.' She gave him the benefit of a stare from the navy blue eyes. It was difficult to interpret whether it was a come-on or a rebuff.

He laughed the conversation on to another tack and they cheerfully talked their way through coq au vin, lemon sorbet, a second bottle of Vouvray, coffee and brandy.

The Castle loomed darkly to their left as they climbed up Johnstone Terrace, but it seemed benign rather than menacing. Charles' arm fitted naturally round the curve of Anna's waist and he could feel the sheen of her skin through the cotton shirt. Edinburgh had regained its magic.

She stopped by a door at the side of a souvenir shop on the Lawnmarket. The city was empty, primly correct, braced for the late-night crowds that the Festival was soon to bring.

'Good Lord, do you live here? A flat full of kilts and whisky shortbread and bagpipe salt-cellars?'

'On the top floor.'

'That's a long way up.'

'A friend's flat. Student at the University here. Away for the summer.'

'Ah. All yours.'

'Yes. Do you want to come in?'

'What for?' Charles asked fatuously.

She was not at all disconcerted and turned the amused navy blue stare on him. 'Coffee?'

'Had coffee.'

'Drink?'

'Had brandy.'

'Well, we'll have to think of something else.'

They did.

CHAPTER FOUR

And the faulty scent is picked out by the hound;
And the fact turns up like a worm from the ground;
And the matter gets wind to waft it about;
And a hint goes abroad and the murder is out.

A TALE OF A TRUMPET

HE WAS ALONE in the bed when he awoke. There was a
note on the pillow. GONE TO REHEARSAL. IF I DON'T
SEE YOU DURING THE DAY, SEE YOU TONIGHT?
He smiled and rolled out of bed to make some leisurely
coffee.

He drank it at the window, looking down on shoppers and
tourists, foreshortened by the distance, scurrying like crabs
across the dark cobbles of the Lawnmarket. He thought of
Anna's brown body with its bikini streaks of white, and felt
good. The cynicism which normally attended his sex life was
not there. An exceptional girl. Willy Mariello's death became
less important.

Rehearsal for an opening in four days' time, on the other
hand, was important. He finished the coffee and set out for
Coates Gardens.

Martin Warburton was sprawled over a camp-bed in the
men's dormitory, reading. Reading *So Much Comic...*,
Charles noticed with annoyance. The boy looked up as he
entered. His expression was calmer than usual and he was
even polite. 'Sorry. I shouldn't be reading this. But it was on
your bed. I started it and got interested.'

Given such a compliment, however unintentional, Charles
could not really complain. 'There's more to Hood than many
people think.'

'I don't know. Is there? I mean he's clever, there's a lot

46

of apparent feeling, but when you get down to it, there's not much there. No certainty. All those puns. It's because he doesn't want to define things exactly. Doesn't want anything to define him. There's nothing you can identify with.'

It was a surprisingly perceptive judgement. 'You think that's important, identifying?'

'It must be. You can only respond to art if you identify with the artist. That's how I worked. I'd read into everything someone had written, until I felt the person there at the centre. And then I'd identify. I'd become that person and know how to react to their work.'

'You're reading English, I assume.'

'No, History.'

'Ah.'

'Just taken my degree.'

'O.K.?'

'Yes, got a First.'

'Congratulations.'

'Not that it means anything.' Martin's mood suddenly gave way to gloom. 'Nothing much does mean anything. I criticise Hood for not believing in things and there's me . . .' He looked up sharply. 'Have you read my play?'

'No, I'm sorry. I will get round to it, but—'

'Wouldn't bother. It's rubbish. Nothing in the middle.'

'I'm sure it's going to be very interesting.' Charles tried not to sound patronising, but was still greeted by a despairing snort. Martin rose suddenly. 'I must go. I'm late. Got to rehearse *Mary*. The composer's body not yet decomposed and we rehearse.'

'You're punning yourself, like Hood,' said Charles, trying to lighten the conversation.

'Oh yes. I'm a punster. A jolly funny punster.' Martin let out one of his abrupt laughs. 'A jolly punster and a murderer. I killed him, you know.'

'No. You were the instrument that killed him.'

This struck Martin as uproariously funny. 'An instrument. Do you want to get into a great discussion about Free Will?

47

Am I guilty? Or is the knife guilty perhaps? Where did the will come from? The knife has no will. I have no will.'

'Martin, calm down. You mustn't think you killed him.'

'Why not? The police think I did.'

'They don't.'

'They asked so many questions.'

'It's the police's job to ask questions.'

'Oh yes, I know.'

'Why? Have you been in trouble with them before?'

'Only a motoring offence, sah!' Martin dropped suddenly into an Irish accent.

'What was it?'

'Planting a car bomb, sah!' He burst into laughter. Charles, feeling foolish for setting up the feed-line so perfectly, joined him. Martin's laughter went on too long.

But Charles took advantage of the slight relaxation of tension. 'Listen, the police can't think you did it. No one in their right mind would commit murder in front of a large audience.'

'No,' said Martin slyly, 'no one in their right mind would.' This again sent him into a paroxysm of laughter. Which stopped as suddenly as it had begun. He looked at Charles in a puzzled way, as if he did not recognise him. Then, in a gentle voice, 'What's the time?'

'Twenty-five to eleven.'

'I should be at rehearsal.' He rose calmly. 'Do try to read my play if you can.'

'I will.'

'See you.' He slouched out of the room.

Charles lay for a moment thinking. Martin seemed to be on the edge of a nervous breakdown. The end of finals is a stressful time for most students. Charles suddenly recalled the state he had been in after Schools in 1949. Three years gone and then the apocalyptic strain of assessment. How good am I? What will I do in the real world? Or, most simply, who am I?

He tried to imagine the effect of a shock like Willy's death

48

on someone in that state. A harsh cruel fact smashing into a mind that could hardly distinguish reality from fantasy. Inside his sick brain Martin might think he was a murderer, but Charles felt sure he was not. Martin Warburton needed help. Medical help possibly, but certainly he needed the help of knowing that he was only an unwitting agent for the person who planned the murder of Willy Mariello. The facts had to come out.

And the show had to go on. He turned to the script. On sober reflection, though the day before's run-through had been promising, there was a lot that needed improvement. Particularly the Pathetic Ballads. They should have been the easiest part of the programme with their well-spaced jokes and obvious humour. But it was hard to find the balance between poetry and facetiousness. He concentrated and began to recite *Tim Turpin*.

> Tim Turpin he was gravel blind,
>   And ne'er had seen the skies :
> For Nature, when his head was made,
>   Forgot to dot his eyes.
> So like a Christmas pedagogue—

'Um. I'm so sorry.' Brian Cassells was peering apologetically round the door.

'Yes?'

'Look, I'm sorry to break into your rehearsal, but I wonder if you could give me a hand to carry something.' And *So Much Comic* . . . was shelved again.

Outside the Office stood Willy Mariello's forlorn guitar in its black case, leaning against a large amplifier. It had been brought up from the Masonic Hall after Tuesday's drama. By the door was a thin girl with long brown hair and those peculiarly Scottish cheeks that really do look like apples. Tension showed in the tightness of her mouth and the hollows under her eyes. 'Charles, this is Jean Mariello. Mrs Mariello, Charles Paris.'

She nodded functionally. 'I've come to collect Willy's things.'

'Yes. Charles, I wonder if you could give me a hand with this amplifier. If we just get it out on to the street, I've phoned for a taxi.'

'O.K.' Brian was patently embarrassed and wanted to get rid of Jean Mariello. His administrative ability did not run to dealing with recent widows.

They placed the heavy amplifier on the pavement. Willy's wife followed with the guitar. Brian straightened up. 'I'd better go. I've got some Letrasetting to get on with.'

'What am I going to do the other end?'

Brian paused, disconcerted by her question. Charles stepped in. 'It's all right. I'll go with you. I wanted to go over that way. Off Lauriston Place, isn't it?'

'Yes.'

'Oh . . . Oh well, that's fine. I'll go and get on with the . . . er . . . Letrasetting.' Brian scuttled indoors.

Charles felt he should say something fitting. 'I'm sorry.'

Jean Mariello shrugged. 'Thank you.'

The taxi arrived and they travelled for a while in silence. Charles felt the need for some other inadequate condolence. 'It must be terrible for you. We were all very shaken.'

'Yes, it's been a shock. But please don't feel you have to say anything. Willy and I weren't love's young dream, you know.' The accent was Scots and she spoke quietly, but there was a hard note in her voice.

'Did you live together?'

'Up to a point. Though one or other of us always seemed to be touring or something.'

'You're a musician too?'

'Yes. I sing in folk clubs. Not Willy's sort of music. We grew apart musically as well as everything else.' She leant forward and tapped the glass partition. 'If you drop us just here . . .'

Meadow Lane was lined with grey houses, considerably smaller than those of Coates Gardens. They had the dusty shabbiness of the Old Town. Most of the windows were shrouded with grey net. But on the house they stopped by the windows were clean and unveiled.

Charles let Jean pay the driver. She turned to him. 'Can you manage that on your own? It's heavy.'

It certainly was. Also an awkward size. His hands could not quite clasp round it. But he was determined to manage.

As she opened the front door, he noticed a worn stone slab over it which dated the house: 1797. Inside, however, the place had been extensively modernised. There was no sign of a fireplace in the front room, but there were new-looking central heating radiators. Everything gleamed with fresh white paint. There was even a smell of it. The room was empty of furniture, but a ladder and a pile of rubble in the corner indicated decorating in progress.

He lowered the amplifier gratefully on to the uncarpeted floor. 'Would you mind putting it against the wall there where people can't see it? The catch has gone on the window and I don't want to encourage burglars.'

Another effort moved the amplifier to the required position. He stood up. Jean Mariello had left the front door open and stood with her arms folded. He was expected to go.

And he was never likely to get such a good opportunity for finding out more about Willy. No point in beating about the bush. 'Mrs Mariello, do you think your husband was murdered?'

She was not shocked or angry, she seemed to expect the question. 'No, I don't.'

'Why not?'

'No one wanted to kill him. Listen, Willy wasn't a particularly nice person. He was mean and lazy. But those aren't reasons for anyone to murder someone.'

'No. But you can't think of anything he might have done to antagonise anyone in that Derby lot?'

'I've hardly met any of that Derby lot, so I wouldn't know. Listen, Mr Paris, I can understand your curiosity, but the police have asked me all these questions and so has everyone

51

I've met for the past two days. I'm getting rather bored with it, and I'd be grateful if you would stop.'

'I'm sorry, Mrs Mariello, but I do have a reason for asking.' And he told her of his encounter with Willy in the Truth Game. At the end he paused dramatically.

She did not seem over-impressed. 'You say he seemed troubled?'

'Yes.'

'Probably some horse he'd backed had been beaten.'

'No, it was more than that. I'm sure it was. Something that really went deep.'

'Nothing went very deep with Willy. That Truth Game could have meant anything. What makes you so sure it was something serious?'

He could only supply a lame 'Instinct'.

To give her her due, Jean Mariello did not actually laugh out loud. 'Well, instinct tells me, from knowing him pretty well, that the only thing that upset Willy was not getting his own way. He was spoilt. He'd had a lot of success and it went to his head. Used to be just a builder's labourer, playing guitar in his spare time. Then the group took off and suddenly he was famous. Everyone gave him everything he wanted and he started getting bad-tempered if anything didn't fall into his lap. If he was upset, it must have been that some girl had slapped his face.'

'There were a lot of girls?'

'Yes.'

'Do you know if he'd been particularly involved with anyone recently?'

'We didn't discuss it. We went our own ways. Listen, Willy was a slob. All right, I'm sorry he died, but he was no great loss.'

Charles was shocked by her honesty and his face must have betrayed it. Jean laughed. 'Yes, you're wondering why I married him. Well, I was only seventeen, I wanted to be a musician and I wanted to get away from my parents. And Willy was different then—it was before he became successful.

He was less sure of himself and, as a result, less selfish. We both changed. He became a bastard and I got a lot tougher. In self-defence.'

There was a slight tremor on the last words, the first sign of human feeling that she had shown. The callous attitude to her husband's death was a protective shell, distancing her from reality. It was true that she had not loved him, but the killing had affected her. Charles changed his approach slightly. 'When did you last see him?'

'Last Friday. I went down to Carlisle to start a tour of folk clubs. Then this happened. I'll be joining the tour again as soon as I've got things sorted out.'

'And Willy didn't seem upset when you left?'

'He was exactly as usual.'

'And you've no idea what he was doing over the weekend?'

'Screwing some bird probably. Decorating here maybe. Rehearsing his bloody show. I don't know.'

The edge was creeping back into her voice. She wanted Charles to leave. She wanted to be on her own. Maybe so that she could break down and cry her heart out. There was not time for many more questions. 'Why did he get involved in the show in the first place?'

'Puce split up. Willy had delusions of grandeur—wanted to get it together as an all-round entertainer. Another Tommy Steele. No big impresario offered him a contract, but Derby University offered him a part in their tatty show. I suppose he saw it as a rung on the ladder to *stardom*.' She put an infinity of scorn into that word.

'Sounds unlikely.'

'Maybe there was some other reason. Look, Mr Paris—'

'I'm sorry. I'll go. Can I just ask you again—was there anyone you can think of, however unlikely, who might have profited by your husband's death?'

'First let me ask you—why are you so interested in all this? It's nothing to do with you.'

'No, you're right, it's just . . . I was there . . . I saw it . . .'

53

He petered out. Tried again. 'There are people who will feel happier when the facts are known. I mean, there's so much gossip and speculation and accusation down at Coates Gardens . . .' As he spoke, he knew it was not true. In fact there had been surprisingly little discussion among the students. Once they had exhausted the inherent drama of the situation, they all seemed quite happy to accept that it was an accident and get back to the more important drama of the shows they were putting on. 'No, I'm sorry, I can't really answer your question.'

'Hmm. I'll answer yours. The only person who stood to benefit from Willy's death was his widow, who would thus get out of an unsatisfactory marriage without the fuss of divorce. In other words, the only person with a motive was me.' She laughed sharply. 'Goodbye, Mr Paris.'

He wandered disconsolately along Meadow Lane and looked back at the house. It was in a better state of repair than the others, walls and chimney repointed, missing slates replaced. And inside, was Jean Mariello as tidy and controlled? Or was she crying? He'd never know. All he did know was that she did not kill her husband. Her talk of motives had just been a contemptuous challenge to him. She had not been in Edinburgh at the time of the murder, and in the Truth Game Willy had specified that the person whose secret he had discovered was connected with the Derby group. No progress.

He felt in need of company. As a long shot, he tried the bell of Anna's flat as he passed. Just after twelve, no reason why she should be there.

She wasn't. He went into the Highland chic of the Ensign Ewart pub opposite and started drinking whisky. As he drank, the whole business of playing at detectives seemed increasingly pointless. If only there were someone around he could discuss the case with. Maybe some great detectives manage on their own, he thought as he downed the second large Bell's, but right now I'd give anything for Dr Watson to walk through that door.

But the Doctor did not come and Charles drank too much on his own. The whisky did not make him think any more clearly. He looked round the pub. The office workers of Edinburgh were in huddles with their backs to him. A loud group of American tourists was being ignored at one table. The Festival influx was not welcomed by the residents. Charles tried to get another drink, but could not attract anyone's attention. Being invisible at a bar is one of the loneliest experiences in life and he felt depressed for the first time since his arrival.

It was the interview with Jean Mariello that had done it. Up until then he had been cheerful, even buoyant after the night with Anna. But Anna was not there and it did not take long for her image to get distorted. He needed her presence to restore reality. But she was as elusive as Dr Watson.

His eyes gave up trying to catch the barman's attention and wandered over to a noticeboard on which the grudging management had stuck a few of the dozens of handbills which earnest theatrical groups had thrust on them. They were on a metal clip. Oxford Theatre Group on top. That was inevitable. Their headquarters was opposite the pub and so they had a head-start on that pitch in the popular Fringe game of sticking your poster over everyone else's.

Beside the Oxford bill was another that looked familiar. Good God, it was one of the greatest D.U.D.S. on the Fringe, Charles Paris' *So Much Comic, So Much Blood*, opening Monday 19th August at one fifteen p.m. He felt a sense of urgency that amounted almost to panic.

'Yes, sir, what can I get you?'

'Nothing. I've got to rehearse.' The barman's bewildered stare followed him out of the pub.

Outside in the street he realised that he had had an excessive lunch for a working actor and trod with care down the steep steps of Lady Stair's Close to the Mound. The light seemed very bright. He thought he saw the familiar figure of Martin Warburton ahead. He hurried to catch up. 'Martin!'

But the figure did not stop. It turned right at the bottom of the steps and Charles saw the beard and glasses. It was not Martin.

He awoke on his camp-bed at about five with the worst sort of afternoon hangover. The urgent rehearsal schedule he had promised himself had petered out rather quickly. He hoped that he had not been seen lying there by too many of the group. A middle-aged man asleep in the afternoon. No doubt snoring. The monotone of the piano upstairs indicated a revue rehearsal. He hoped Anna had not seen him.

A cup of coffee might help. He eased himself downstairs to the kitchen. The day's cook, a large girl with corkscrew curls, was chopping up more of the inevitable cabbage.

'Where's the coffee?'

'Over there, behind the cornflakes.'

'Oh yes.'

'I'll make you some . . .'

'Thanks.' He made to sit on a chair by the table.

'. . . if you don't mind doing something for me.'

'What?'

'Just empty that, would you?'

'That' was a large cardboard box full of rubbish—papers, sweepings, cigarette ends, kitchen refuse. The bottom felt unwholesomely soggy on his hands. Charles Paris, haulage contractors. Amplifiers, refuse—distance no object. He negotiated the load through the kitchen door and made his way to the dustbins.

There was a little room at the top of one of them. He balanced the box on the edge and tried to let the contents slip gently in.

They all came with a rush, covering his hands with tea-leaves and a yellow slime that had been food. Little scraps of paper scattered all around the bin.

He pushed down the smelly pile and bent to pick up some of the litter. A lot of the paper appeared to have been torn from a big poster photograph. He picked up a piece which had printing on it.

WI
PU

He scrabbled among the other bits until he found the adjacent one which spelled out the title.

WILLY MARIELLO
PUCE

It was a publicity poster of Willy that someone had shredded into a thousand pieces.

CHAPTER FIVE

How bless'd the heart that has a friend
A sympathising ear to lend
   To troubles too great to smother!
For as ale and porter, when flat, are restored
Till a sparkling bubbling head they afford,
So sorrow is cheer'd by being poured
   From one vessel to another.

MISS KILMANSEGG AND HER PRECIOUS LEG

FROM BIBLICAL TIMES the restorative properties of a young woman's body have been acknowledged, and Charles felt better after another night with Anna. He was amazed how much she affected him. She was beautiful, and she was knowledgeable in bed, but it was not just that. There was something about the honesty of her responses. No extravagant protestations of love, no questions about the future, just an acceptance that what was happening was good. Most people reveal their weaknesses in a close relationship and endear themselves by failure. But the nearer Charles got to Anna the more complete and integrated she seemed. And she made him feel complete too. Not two lost souls leaning against each other for support, but two independent people who complemented each other.

The alarm woke them at nine. Charles reached his hand round to the small of her back and kissed the elastic skin of her breasts. Anna smiled. 'Got to get up.'

'Saturday.'

'No weekend for us. The revue opens on Monday. We've got a tech. run at ten.'

'Yes, the show must go on.' She got up. Charles squatted ruefully on the bed with his elbows on his knees. Anna

58

paused in the bathroom doorway and grinned. 'You look like a dog that's had its bone taken away.'

'Yes, I fancied a nice bit of marrow-bone jelly. Isn't that what Prolongs Active Life?'

'You needn't worry.' She closed the bathroom door. Charles smiled, gratified. He spoke up over the sound of running water. 'Hey, look, I've got a lot of rehearsal to do, too. Can I use the flat? It's so difficult to find anywhere quiet at Coates Gardens.'

A gurgle from the bathroom gave him permission. 'What are the technical lot like, Anna? All the sound and lighting people?' Another gurgle said they were fine, there was a good course in the Department of Drama. 'I hope so. I'm only getting a few hours' rehearsal in the hall—Sunday and Monday morning is all I'm allowed.'

The bathroom door slid open and Anna appeared, naked, her hair spiked with damp. 'Not fair, is it, you poor old thing?' she said as she crossed to her clothes on the chair.

He grabbed at her ankle as she passed and she flopped on to the bed. 'Got to go and rehearse, Charles.'

'Rehearse and become a big star.'

'Yes.'

'Even stars have five minutes.'

The rehearsal went well too. Given somewhere to work on his own, Charles concentrated and put more subtlety into his readings. He was very organised. Once straight through, then a laborious line-by-line analysis of what had gone wrong. Another run—improvements in individual items but too uniform a pace overall. More detailed work, and finally a run that he would not have been ashamed to show to an audience. 'There are many pleasures to be had at the Edinburgh Festival, and the greatest of these is Charles Paris' *So Much Comic, So Much Blood*.' Silly, however old and cynical he got, there were times when his mind raced and fantasies of success made him deliciously nervy and excited.

After rehearsal he found the pubs were shut and that

made him feel virtuous. A brisk walk was called for. He popped into a little café aptly called the Poppin and bought a couple of floury ham rolls. Then started a leisurely stroll up to the Castle.

The Esplanade was flanked with tiers of seats ready for the Military Tattoo. The head of a statue and the point of an obelisk came up through the disciplined rows to be capped incongruously by green tarpaulin covers. But the Castle itself still looked impressive as Charles mounted the gentle incline to its heraldic gateway. 'Nemo me impune lacessit.' The motto's translation came to his mind in the accent of a Glasgow thug—'No one provokes me and gets away with it.'

It was like a pilgrimage. Every time he came up to Edinburgh, he had to look round the Castle. Climb up to Mons Meg, maybe look inside St Margaret's Chapel. Then on the level below he would lean against the ramparts and gaze down over the city, whose greys merged to distant greens, which were lost in the gleam of the Firth of Forth.

It was a clear, sparkling day. He had a beautiful girl and he felt confident about his show. And yet . . .

And yet there was a nagging unease in his mind. Willy Mariello's murder. Each time he tried to dismiss it, he saw the fear in those brown eyes. And he knew that the pleasures of Edinburgh could only allay his unrest temporarily. Peace would not come until he knew the full facts.

The facts he had found out did not take him far. There were still some forty suspects who had had equal opportunity to switch the knives. Of those two had had greater opportunities than the others to stage-manage the murder— Martin Warburton and Pam Northcliffe. Martin had struck the fatal blow and he was an unstable character with strange obsessions about violence. But it seemed too obvious, and Charles felt an understanding, even an affinity with the boy's tormented mind. He could not think of him as a murderer.

The same applied to Pam. However, it was she who had actually issued the murder weapon and there were other strange features of her behaviour. He had a strong suspicion that she was responsible for the torn poster. The pieces that he had found had burst out of a paper bag full of crêpe paper scraps which Pam had been using to make props. He had not challenged her with it, but he was fairly certain. So she had something to hide.

But not murder. Why not? Because I, Charles Paris, like the girl. The same goes for Martin. It is a hopelessly subjective, emotional judgement. I have an old-fashioned, middle-class view that murderers are, by definition, nasty people. Whereas, in fact, they are just nice, ordinary people who get into situations they can't cope with and take what seems to them the only way out.

Again he desperately wanted someone to talk to about his suspicions. Someone detached and objective. Not Anna. She was involved with the other students and he did not want the murder to intrude on their growing relationship. But there was always Gerald.

Gerald Venables was a show business solicitor with a child-like relish for the cloak and dagger aspect of detection. Charles had enlisted his help earlier in the year to sort out the Marius Steen affair and, when that mystery was solved, Gerald had insisted that he should be included in any future venture of criminal investigation. This looked like his opportunity.

'Hello, Gerald.'
'Who's that? Charles?'
'Yes. I think I may be on to another case.'
'Really.' Excitement sprang into Gerald's voice. 'Where?'
'Edinburgh, I'm afraid. It'd cost you a lot in fares.'
'Don't worry. I've got lots of Scottish clients. I can put it on one of their bills. What's the crime?'
'Murder.'
'Fantastic. Will it keep?'
'What do you mean?'

'Keep for a few days. I'm going to Cannes for a long weekend to stay with a client.'

'Work?'

'Well, it'll be on his bill, but I don't intend to do anything.'

'When are you back?'

'Probably Wednesday.'

'Some weekend.'

'Pity to rush it.'

'Hmm.' Wednesday seemed a long way off. Charles wanted someone there to talk to at that moment.

Gerald continued. 'And then at the end of next week—Saturday—I'm taking the family out to our villa in Corsica for a month.'

'Just the month?'

'Yes. I have to get back to work then,' said Gerald piously, not catching Charles' sarcasm.

'So you might be free for a couple of days next week?'

'Might. The case won't be solved by then, will it?'

'No, I shouldn't think so.' Depression swooped and Charles feared he was speaking the truth. 'I'll give you a buzz when you get back if there's anything left to investigate. O.K. Fine. Have a good weekend.' It was not worth saying how pointless it would be for Gerald to come up for two days. Oh, well, another good idea gone west.

'Oh, it's you, Charles.' James Milne was standing at the foot of the stairs in the hall. 'I wondered who was using the phone. That one's just an extension to mine upstairs. It's meant to be disconnected soon and I'd put it in the cupboard so that it shouldn't be used.'

'I'm sorry. It was just here on the floor when I came in.'

'Don't worry. One of the Derby lot found it, no doubt. How's Thomas Hood?'

'Fine. Positively going well.'

'Good, good.' The Laird stood with one foot on the stair, posed like an old-fashioned print. His stocky figure was dressed in a biscuit-coloured tweed suit with a Norfolk jacket. 'Can I offer you a cup of tea?'

A slow grin spread over Charles's face. 'Dr Watson,' he said.

'I beg your pardon.'

Over a cup of Earl Grey tea and chocolate-covered Bath Olivers, Charles explained. He told of his suspicions about the murder and the small progress of his investigations.

James Milne looked at him in silence for a moment. 'What an amazing idea. And what do you want me to do? Crawl around the rooftops with firearms and beard villains in their dens? I don't know whether that's quite my style. I used sometimes to try to catch poachers on my mother's estate at Glenloan, but I'm not exactly a private eye.'

'Look, all I want you to do is to address your mind to the problem. I want to hear what you think. You've met most of the people involved. You know, two heads are better than one and all that. And I'm really getting nowhere on my own. My suspicions just go round and round in circles . . . I want you to be a kind of sounding board for my ideas.'

'Hmm. I think a ouija board for contacting Willy Mariello might be more useful.'

'You're probably right. What do you say?'

'Well, Charles, I'm certainly prepared to help you in any way you think might be useful. But I must say right from the start that I don't share your certainty that a murder has been committed. From what I heard it sounded like a very unfortunate accident. What makes you so sure it's murder?'

Again Charles had to fall back on his feeble cry of 'Instinct'.

' "Instinct is a great matter, I was a coward on instinct." Hmm. Dear old Falstaff. Instinct. Do the police share your instinct?'

'Not so far as I know.'

'They don't think it was murder?'

'I don't think so, though that won't really be clear until they've finished their enquiries.'

'No. Hmm. Good.'

'Why good?'

'Well, when our investigations reach their dramatic dénouement, we can feel confident that Inspector Flatfoot of the Yard won't pip us at the post.'

'You mean you agree?'

'Yes, I'll be your sounding board. It could be fun.'

'Good. Thank you.'

The Laird immediately regressed to his school-mastering days. 'Right. Now have you made any notes on the case?'

'No.'

'Well, I'm sure you should.' Charles watched amazed as his Dr Watson began to organise him. 'Right, paper, fountain pen, sharp HB pencil. And a column, so. Headed 'Suspects'. And another—'Reason for Suspicion'. Now who have we got?'

'We've just been through all that.'

'No harm in doing it again. There is nothing so effective for stimulating the memory and provoking thought as writing things down.'

Charles felt he was right back in the First Form. (On his present investigative form, in the corner with a big 'D' on his hat.) But he humoured his new partner and they made out their list.

It did not take long. The 'Reason for Suspicion' column looked particularly unconvincing. 'In a sense,' said Charles, 'we're starting from the wrong end. We are putting down why we suspect someone, whereas we should be thinking, from that person's point of view, why they should want to kill Willy.'

'Would that make the list any fuller?'

Charles had to admit that it would not. 'What we've got to do is to work out who was involved with Willy—emotionally, artistically, financially. So far it seems the only person from Derby he knew well is a guy called Sam Wasserman, who is currently touring Europe.'

'You say he's the only person you can connect Willy with?'

'Except for his wife. But I can't count her because she has

64

nothing to do with the group. Unless she has an ally who's at Derby . . . A lover maybe or . . .' Lack of conviction in what he was saying brought him to a halt. 'Nope.'

'And she's the only person up here with whom he seems to have had dealings?'

'Yes.'

'Oh, Charles, Charles.' The Laird shook his head pityingly. 'There's someone you've overlooked.'

'Is there?'

'Yes. And you have all the information to work out who. I know you do.' He watched for reaction and then repeated slowly, 'I know you do.'

Charles suddenly realised who was meant. 'Good Lord, yes. You. The house.'

'Exactly. You see, there is a direct financial relationship between me and Willy Mariello. He bought my house. I think I should go down on our list of suspects.'

'But that's daft. If you were the murderer, you wouldn't draw my attention to your connection with the victim.'

'Ah, Charles, I may look like the innocent flower, but be the serpent under't. You mustn't rule out any possibility. There, I've put my name down. Declaration of interests, like the Liberals keep asking M.P.s to make. Now what about you?'

'Me?'

'Your declaration of interest. Had you any motive to murder Willy Mariello?'

Charles laughed. 'No.'

'Good. Now we know where we stand.' James Milne smiled. His reserve was gone and he looked set to enjoy the game of detection. 'Now, what about the other forty-odd?'

'What indeed? Presumably I must try to meet them all and find out if any of them knew Willy well. And also what he did over the weekend before he died.'

'Yes. And how long have you got to complete this major investigation?'

'My show finishes a week today.'

'Hmm. I fear we may find time defeats us.'

'Yes. I hope not.'

'So do I. But perhaps, Charles, I hope it a little less than you.'

'Why?'

'Because I don't yet fully believe that we're on to a case of murder. I'll come along with you for the ride, but I'm not convinced of the existence of a destination.'

The Laird was going to dinner with friends, so Charles left him about seven. He was no nearer the solution of the murder, but at least he had an ally. And the cataloguing power of James Milne's mind could be a useful complement to his own haphazard methods.

On the first-floor landing he paused. The revue piano had given up its usual stuck-in-the-groove repetition and was playing a whole tune. A girl was singing. He could not catch the lyrics, just hear the husky purity of her voice. Anna. He felt a strong desire to go into the room on some pretext just to see her. But no. She had said it was better they should keep their relationship a secret and she was right. He did not fancy the gossip and innuendo of forty students.

No. He still had the key to the flat. He'd go back there and wait for her to return and continue his rejuvenation. Later.

On the ground floor the only sign of human occupation was the presence of old socks, creeping like firedamp from the men's dormitory. Charles was about to leave and find a pub for the evening when he heard a slight sound from the basement. He crept down the stairs towards the glow of the sitting-room.

Michael Vanderzee was slumped on the sofa with a glass in one hand and a half-full bottle of Glenmorangie malt whisky in the other. He perceived Charles's approach blearily. 'I didn't know there was anyone in the house. Thought they'd all buggered off.'

'I've just been having a drink with the Laird.'

'Oh, that old poof,' said Michael ungraciously.

Charles did not bother to challenge the gratuitous insult, though on reflection he thought it was misplaced. He had not thought before about James Milne's sexual status, but, when he did, neuter seemed the most appropriate definition.

However, Michael was not trying to drive Charles away. On the contrary, he seemed delighted to have a witness of his lonely drinking and an audience for his self-pity.

'Charles Paris, you may work in bullshit commercial theatre, but at least you are a professional.' The drink accentuated the Dutchness of his voice as he delivered this back-handed compliment. 'Surrounded by bloody amateurs in this place. It's an impossible situation for any creative work. You can't create with amateurs.'

Charles grunted sympathetically and sat astride a chair. 'Have a drink,' said Michael, feeling that perhaps he should offer his audience some reward for its attention. 'There's a cup on the table.'

The cup was chipped and handleless, but the malt tasted good. When he reckoned that Charles was sitting comfortably, Michael began. 'No, I shouldn't have taken this job. Amateurs have no concept of theatre. Look at it. This evening I should have been working, improvising, creating something, and what happens? Half my cast are rehearsing for some bloody revue, half of them are doing some dreary Shakespeare crap, half of them aren't interested . . .'

'And half of them get stabbed . . .'

'Yes.' He nodded vigorously. 'Though he wasn't a lot more use to me when he was alive.'

'What do you mean?'

'Never came to bloody rehearsals. Didn't participate in the concentration exercises or movement classes, any of the workshop stuff. I mean, how can you build an ensemble with people like that? He hadn't any acting talent anyway.'

'Then why did you cast him in your show?'

'I didn't cast him. Look, I'm offered this job—'

'You mean you're nothing to do with the university?'

67

'Good God, no.' Michael was severely affronted. 'I'm a professional director. They booked me to get some professional feel into their production. And then like bloody amateurs they don't give me enough time to get it together properly. Everyone off for other rehearsals. Do you know how long it takes to build up an ensemble?'

'About four years?'

'Well, four weeks anyway. And four weeks' work. Not four weeks doing bourgeois revues and middle-class Shakespeare.'

'No, of course not. You were saying how Willy Mariello came to be in the show . . .'

'Yes. O.K., I take the job. I go to Derby to hold auditions. And already I'm told that Willy is doing the music and, since Rizzio's a guitarist and he has a couple of songs, O.K., he's playing Rizzio too.'

'Who told you this?'

'Sam Wasserman, the guy who wrote this crappy play.'

'Is it crappy?'

'Yes, but it doesn't matter.'

'Why not?'

'My style of direction doesn't need a good play. In fact the play can get in the way. It's only a starting point from which the totality emerges—the iron filing dropped into the acid which produces the perfect crystal.' He added the last image with great satisfaction, albeit dubious chemistry. Then he looked at Charles with pitying contempt. 'I suppose you still think a play has got to have words.'

Charles smiled apologetically. There was no point in alienating such a ready source of information. 'Yes, I am a bit of an old fuddy-duddy on that score. I expect Sam Wasserman probably thinks words are quite important too.'

'Maybe.'

'He sounds an interesting bloke. I'd like to meet him.'

Michael gave a snort of laughter that could have meant anything. 'You should get a chance quite soon. He's coming up to Edinburgh.'

'For the opening in the Third Week?'

'No, before that, I hope. We've been sending telegrams all over Europe for him. He's going to come up and take over the part of Rizzio.'

'Oh really.' That was very interesting. 'He plays guitar too?'

'Yes. He was going to do the music for the show himself until Willy was brought in.'

'Ah.' That was also interesting. 'So everything's back to where it started?'

'I suppose so. More drink?'

'Thank you.' Charles held out his cup and the malt was sloshed in like school soup. Trying desperately to sound casual, he asked, 'What did you think of Willy Mariello?'

'Useless, unco-operative bastard. Ruining my production. From my point of view, his death was the best thing that could have happened.'

It was an uncompromising statement of hatred. So much so that Charles felt inclined to discount it. A murderer would be more guarded . . . Unless it was an elaborate double bluff . . . Oh dear. The further he got into the business of detection, the further certainty seemed to recede. Still, keep on probing. Try to find out some more hard facts. Again he imposed a relaxed tone on his voice. 'Were you rehearsing last weekend?'

'Of course. I rehearse whenever I can get my cast together. I am trying to create something, you know.'

'Of course. So Willy was rehearsing all weekend?'

'No. That's a good example of what I mean. He rehearses on Saturday with his usual bad grace. Sunday—no sign of him. Monday he is not there and I am so furious I break the rehearsal and I go up to his house to drag him back— by force if necessary.'

'Was he there?'

'Oh yes, he's there. Calmly decorating. Plaster dust everywhere, paint brushes, so on and so on.'

'Did you get him to rehearsal?'

'Yes, till mid-afternoon. Then he slipped off again when we had a break.'

'Hmm. Perhaps he wanted to get back to his decorating.'

'Yes. Or to the girl.'

'Girl?'

'Yes. When I finally got him out on the Monday morning, he called out 'Goodbye' to someone upstairs.'

CHAPTER SIX

In they go—in jackets, and cloaks,
Plumes, and bonnets, turbans and toques,
    As if to a Congress of Nations :
Greeks and Malays, with daggers and dirks,
Spaniards, Jews, Chinese, and Turks—
Some like original foreign works,
    But mostly like bad translations.

MISS KILMANSEGG AND HER PRECIOUS LEG

By Sunday 18th August Edinburgh was beginning to feel the Festival. Over-night the city was full of tourists— tweedy music-lovers on leisurely promenades, earnest Americans decked with rucksacks and guide-books, French and Japanese drawn by the twin attractions of culture and Marks and Spencer pullovers. The residents who had not escaped on holiday wore expressions of resignation, hardened to the idea of their streets clogged with ambling foreigners, their early nights troubled by returning revue audiences and the distant massed pipes and drums of the Military Tattoo.

Because that Sunday was the day when it all started officially. In the words of the Festival brochure, 'The twenty-eighth Edinburgh Festival will be opened with a Service of Praise and Thanksgiving in St Giles' Cathedral on Sunday 18th August at 3 p.m. Later, starting from the Castle Esplanade at 9.45 p.m., relays of torch-bearing runners will light a bonfire on Arthur's Seat.'

And in the little halls of Edinburgh on that Sunday morning would-be cultural torch-bearers blew earnestly at the smoulderings of what was in many cases incombustible material. Experimental and university groups realised that their rehearsal time was running out and put on a spurt to

71

justify the extravagant claims of their publicity. There were dress rehearsals for at least a dozen 'funniest revues on the Fringe', some twenty 'revolutionary new plays', and three or four 'new artistic concepts which would flatten the accepted barriers of culture'. If all these ambitions were realised, British theatre would never be the same again.

In the Masonic Hall in Lauriston Street Charles Paris was trying to realise more humble ambitions and finding it hard work. The lighting technician he had been allocated was a fat and contemptuous youth, whose blue denim had faded and dirtied to the colour of sludge. He was known as Plug, and Charles found it difficult to call anyone 'Plug'.

It had been made clear that, considering the exacting demands of creative amateur theatre, there was not going to be much time or effort left for him, a mere professional. 'Um . . . Plug?' he said exploratively, 'I wonder about the chances of moving the back-projector round. If it stays there, I'm going to be masking the slides.'

'That'd mean moving the screen too,' Plug grunted accusingly.

'Yes, it will.'

'Can't be done. Haven't got the extension leads.'

'Can't you get them?'

'Shouldn't think so.'

Charles bit back his anger. It was difficult dealing with amateurs. In a professional context, no problem; he could have bawled the guy out, justified because a service that was being paid for was not being provided. But the amateur relies on goodwill and there did not seem to be much of it in evidence.

So he gritted his teeth and played stupid, apparently bowing to Plug's technical expertise and working the youth round till he did what was required as a demonstration of his abilities. It was important, Charles had gone to considerable trouble to have slides made of Hood's woodcuts. They had originally been printed with the poems and the crude humour of the pictures extended the range of the verse.

In a one-man show it is important to give the audience as much varied stimulus as possible.

By application of simple child psychology he got the back-projector and screen moved and started a run. It was not easy. With only two stage areas in use, the lighting plot was simple. But Plug refused to rehearse the cues on their own, saying that he would pick them up on a full run. Then, in spite of the carefully marked-up script that Charles had given him, he proceeded to get every single effect wrong.

The one benefit of the run was that it tested Charles' knowledge of his words, because whether he moved to the table or the lectern, there was a guarantee of total darkness on that area. And whenever he turned to the back-projection screen, he was confronted either by a blank or the wrong slide.

It was also a useful concentration exercise. In the darkness beyond the stage people kept wandering in and out. Plug greeted them all loudly and conducted irrelevant conversations at the top of his voice. Charles was ignored like a television in the corner of the room.

The show limped to its close. As he stood at the lectern to read the final *Stanzas*, 'Farewell, Life! My senses swim ...', he was amazed to find the light was actually where it should be. It had taken the whole show to get one cue right, but at least it offered hope. Encouraged, he put more emotion into the poem. It approached its end with the dying fall he had intended.

> 'O'er the earth there comes a bloom—
> Sunny light for sullen gloom,
> Warm perfume for vapour cold—'

then, before 'I smell the Rose above the Mould', the pause held long and dramatic.

Too long. Too dramatic. Plug snapped the lights out before the line was delivered.

Charles's reserves cracked. 'Oh, for Christ's sake!'

'What's up?' Plug grunted from the darkness.

'That's not the cue. There's another line.'

Plug did not seem unduly concerned. He brought up the house lights. 'Never mind.'

'And then, after the last line, there's supposed to be a three-second pause and a five-second fade down to black.'

'Oh.'

'It's clearly marked in the script.'

'Yes.'

Charles decided there was little point in concealing his feelings. 'That was pretty abysmal.'

Plug nodded sympathetically, unaware that the comment referred to him. 'Hmm. Perhaps you need more rehearsal.'

'I think it's you who needs more rehearsal. None of the cues were right.'

Plug's silence indicated that this was an unworthy attack on his life work. Charles continued, 'So let's have one run-through of just the cues and then do the whole show again.'

'There's not much point.'

'Why not? The show opens tomorrow.'

'Yes, but I won't be doing the lights then. I'm only here for the rehearsal.'

Charles tried to find out what would be happening about his lights in the actual show from the Company Manager, and Brian Cassells was confident that everything would be all right. Charles, who found Brian's confidence increasingly unnerving, was not convinced.

'Oh, incidentally, Charles, will you be going down to the Fringe reception?'

'What's that?'

'At five o'clock. Royal Mile Centre. It's sort of to launch everything. You know, Press'll be there and all that.'

'Then I'll certainly come.' Any chance of publicity must be taken. He was not too optimistic of the 'D.U.D.S. of the Fringe' poster bringing audiences flocking to see him.

Since the pubs were not open on Sunday, he had cabbage lunch with the rest of the group. The conversation was all of the coming shows. Willy Mariello's death had been almost forgotten. Charles looked round the table. Anna was not there. He suddenly wished she was, or wished that he was with her somewhere keeping the blues at bay.

The loud T-shirted crowd joked and attitudinised. He felt old and envious. Their values were so simple. What they were doing on the Fringe was the most important thing that had ever happened; that was all there was to it. Their shows consumed all their thoughts and energies.

Except for the thoughts of one person—the murderer. He or she must be feeling regret or anxiety or something. But the lunchtime crowd showed no signs of guilty conscience. They all seemed interchangeably brash and cheerful. Pam Northcliffe was up the far end of the table as nervously bright and giggly as the rest. Communal excitement had replaced the short tempers of earlier in the week.

Martin Warburton was not there. Charles wondered if he would be sharing in the group gaiety if he were. There was still a lot to be found out about Martin Warburton. That afternoon might be a good opportunity to read *Who Now?* —a Disturbing New Play.

It was disturbing. The language was good, there was some sense of structure, but the content was frightening. As the title implied, questions of identity figured large. None of the characters seemed to have a fixed personality; they were chameleons who took on the colour of different forms of violence. There was a woolly Leftish political message coming through the monologues that made up the play. Its main tenet seemed to be that, come the Revolution, the bourgeois would be destroyed. But it was the way in which they were going to be destroyed that was disturbing. Images of bombings, secret beatings and firing squads abounded. Continually blood welled, bones cracked, corpses twitched and entrails spilled. So much blood.

Under normal circumstances, Charles would have put it down to over-writing. Some of the extended metaphors even

75

reminded him of his own adolescent literary excesses. But even so, and even given a young person's insensitive ignorance of the real facts of death, there was something obsessive about the play. A morbid preoccupation with violence unbalanced the writer's considerable natural talent.

And became uncomfortably relevant in the light of Willy Mariello's death.

About half past four Martin Warburton suddenly appeared in the men's dormitory. He seemed in a hurry and had dropped in to collect something from his suitcase. Charles was lying on his camp-bed checking through *So Much Comic* ...

'Oh, Martin, I've read your play.'

'Ah.' He seemed embarrassed.

'I'd like to talk about it.'

'Ah.'

'Now? If you're walking down to this reception, we could chat on the way.'

'I'm not going to the reception.' Martin hesitated. He was improvising. 'I'm going to meet someone down at ... er ... Dean Village.'

'Oh. O.K. Well, some other time.'

'Yes.'

Charles started off with some of the *Mary* cast to walk to the Royal Mile Centre. Just as they were about to cross Princes Street to go up the Mound, he realised that he had not brought any of his hand-outs. Even a playbill offering one of the DUDS of the Fringe was better than no publicity. Brian Cassells would not have thought to take any. With some annoyance, because it was a warm afternoon, he started back along Princes Street.

He was waiting for the lights to cross Charlotte Street when he saw Martin over the other side striding purposefully along Lothian Road. In the opposite direction from Dean Village.

Charles was not aware of making the decision, but it seemed natural to cross over Princes Street and follow. He was some fifty yards behind his quarry and there were enough meandering tourists about to make the pursuit look casual. He kept his eyes fixed on the blue denim back ahead.

Martin turned left along Castle Terrace which skirts the great Castle rock, then crossed over Spittal Street and climbed up towards Lauriston Place. Maybe going to the Masonic Hall. The scene of the crime. There were no rehearsals that afternoon. Everyone was going down to the reception. Or perhaps Martin was aiming for the Mariello's house in Meadow Lane. Charles felt a spurt of excitement.

There were less people about in this part of the old town, so he dawdled. He did not want to be noticed if Martin stopped suddenly.

But the boy did not stop. The blue denim back continued its progress. Past the Masonic Hall, no hesitation. Past the Meadow Lane turning. On past the Infirmary, looking neither left nor right. Charles began to feel it was a long walk.

And it continued. On past the University Union with its cloth banner advertising Russell Hunter in *Knox*. On to Nicholson Square and then suddenly right, along the broad pavement of Nicholson Street. Martin still kept up his even, preoccupied pace, with Charles alternately lingering and hurrying along behind.

The whole thing seemed pointless. Charles could not really think what he was doing, playing this elaborate game of cops and robbers when he should be snatching much-needed publicity at the reception. Perhaps Martin was just going out for a walk. Something innocuous. Something—

Martin had disappeared. The fact jerked Charles out of his reverie. One moment the denim back had been moving smoothly along, the next it was gone. In the middle of a parade of shops. No chance of having turned up a side street.

Cautiously Charles moved forward to where he had last seen Martin. All the shops were Sunday shut. Their fronts were separated by doors which served the flats above. Gently

77

Charles pushed the one nearest to where he had last seen Martin.

It was a heavy door, but it gave. The stone hall was dark and suddenly cool. A pram. A bicycle. Stone stairs, a metal rail. And attached to the top of the door a heavy chain that was part of some antiquated system to open it from the flats above.

Just an ordinary hall of an ordinary tenement block. Silence. He could not start barging into private flats at high tea time on an Edinburgh Sunday afternoon. Anyway, what was he looking for? He went out into the street again.

The names on the old-fashioned bell-pushes told him nothing. McHarg, Stewart, Grant, Wilson. He waited for about five minutes, apparently intrigued by a display of dusty Pyrex in an adjacent shop. Martin did not re-emerge. It was after half past five. Charles set off for the Royal Mile Centre.

At the entrance he was asked to identify himself.

'Charles Paris.'

'Not your name. Who are you with?'

'Oh, Derby University Dramatic Society.'

The result was that he entered the upstairs assembly room with a red card badge bearing the legend 'D.U.D.S.'. It did not seem very positive advertising.

Entering the room was difficult; it was so full that he had to ease one shoulder in as a wedge and wriggle the rest of his body in after it. Some people had glasses of drink. Infallible instinct tracked its source and he slid and sidled over to a long table.

The drink was a pink wine-cup of minimal alcoholic content. Charles looked out across the throng. A swarm of cultural locusts was buzzing loudly and milling round the red badges which bore the names of newspapers, radio or television companies.

Everyone had a badge. *Radio Clyde* bounced on the forceful breasts of a young reporter. *Bradford* clung to chain

78

mail worn to publicise their play *The Quest. B.B.C.* flopped on well-cut mohair. *Nottingham* sagged on a dirty T-shirt.

And everyone forced literature on everyone else. Charles had only to stand there to become a litter-bin for hand-outs and programmes. He kicked himself for wasting time following Martin and not getting his own publicity.

A glance at the cultural treats the literature offered revealed that there was not much he would want to see, but it was at least varied. There was *Problem 32* by Framework Theatre—'ten young designers creating an hour's theatre in their own terms'. The World Première of *Scots Wha Hae*, a new Scots comedy from the group that brought you *The De'il's Awa'* and *Cambusdonald Royal*. Paris Pandemonium Projects offered *Chaos, Un Collage de Comédie*. Under the intriguing title *Charlotte Brontë and her Scotsmen*, Accolade were presenting 'psychological deduction of her relations with men in her last years (reduced prices for students and Old Age Pensioners)'. Or there was Birkenhead Dada with *We Call for the Decease of Salvador Dali*—'Shocks, poems and perversions; indefensible personal attacks; new levels of tastelessness.'

In other words the Fringe was much as usual. But with decreasing conviction. Charles remembered the heady days of the late fifties and early sixties when Edinburgh was the only outlet for experimental drama in Britain. The recent spread of little theatres in London and other major cities had eroded that unique position. And the Edinburgh Fringe seemed less important. Less truly experimental. Too many of the university groups were doing end-of-term productions of classics rather than looking for new ideas.

'Not a lot, is there, Charles?'

He looked up and recognised one of the *Guardian* critics. 'Just thinking the same. How long are you up?'

'A week. A week of sifting dirty sand looking for diamonds. Which probably don't exist.'

'Sounds fun.'

'But what are you doing up here?'

'My one-man show on Thomas Hood. *So Much Comic, So Much Blood.*'

'Oh, I'd like to see that. Did it at York, didn't you?'

'Yes.'

'Hmm. I missed it there. Haven't seen much publicity.'

'No, it's been a bit thin on the ground. Last-minute booking.'

'Ah. Well, give me the details.' The critic wrote them down on the back of a Theatre Wagon of Virginia, U.S.A. handout that looked depressingly disposable. 'Right, I'll be along.'

'And spread the word among your colleagues. Or rivals.'

'Will do, Charles.' The critic edged off into the throng.

It might be worth something. But he should have brought the hand-outs. His own printed sheet stood more chance of survival than jottings on the back of someone else's.

The crush got worse rather than better. Over on the far side of the room Anna's cropped head was instantly recognisable. She was talking enthusiastically, surrounded by a crowd of journalists. He felt a momentary pang of jealousy, a desire to go over and claim her. But no, she was right. Better to keep it quiet. Later they'd be together. The thought warmed him.

'Hello.' Pam Northcliffe wormed her way between a green velvet suit and a coat of dishcloth chain mail. She looked flushed and breathless. There was an empty glass in her hand which Charles filled from a jug on the table. 'Oh Lord.' She took a sip at it. 'A few people, aren't there?'

'Just a few. How are you?'

'Oh. Pissed, I think.' She giggled at the audacity of her vocabulary. He was surprised. He felt he could have poured that pink fluid into himself for a year and not registered on the most sensitive breathalyser. Still, Pam claimed to be pissed and certainly she was much more relaxed and forthcoming on what she thought of her fellow-students. A wicked humour flashed into her observations and at times she even looked attractive.

Charles decided that this confidential mood was too good

to waste from the point of view of his investigations. The crowd was beginning to thin out, but he did not want to lose her. 'You rehearsing now?'

'No, they're doing the *Dream* at seven thirty—a run as per performance. I'll be doing props for the revue at eleven —if I'm sober enough.'

'Come and have another drink. That'll sober you up.'

She giggled. 'Everywhere's closed on a Sunday.'

'No. We can go up to the Traverse.'

The Traverse Theatre Club had moved since Charles had last been there doing a strange Dürrenmatt play in 1968. But he found the new premises and managed to re-establish his membership. (The girl on the box-office was distrustful until he explained his credentials as a genuine actor and culture-lover. Too many people tried to join for the club's relaxed drinking hours rather than its theatrical milestones.)

The media contingent from the Royal Mile Centre seemed to have been transplanted bodily to the Traverse bar. But the crush was less and Charles and Pam found a round wooden table to sit on. He fought to the counter and brought back two glasses of red wine as trophies. 'Cheers, Pam.'

'Cheers.' She took a long swallow. Then she looked at him. 'Thank you.'

'What for?'

'Bringing me here.'

'It's nothing.'

'No, it's kind of you. I know it's only because you feel sorry for me.'

'Well, I . . .' He was embarrassed. He had not done it for that reason, but his real motive was not much more defensible. 'What do you mean?'

'You're just being kind. Taking me out of myself. And I appreciate it.' She spoke without rancour. 'I know I'm not very attractive.'

He laughed uneasily. 'Oh, come on. What's that got to do with it? I mean, not that you aren't attractive, but I mean . . . Can't I just ask you for a drink because I like your company? Do you take me for a dirty old man? I'm old enough to be your father.' (And, incidentally, old enough to be Anna's father.)

He was floundering. Fortunately Pam did not seem to notice; she wanted to talk about her predicament. 'I never realised how important being pretty was. When I lived at home, my parents kept saying I was all right and I suppose I believed them. Then, when I went to Derby, all that was taken away. What you looked like was the only thing that mattered and I was ugly.' Charles could not think of anything helpful to say. She seemed quite rational, not self-pitying, glad of an audience. She continued, 'You had to have a man.'

'Or at least fancy one?'

'Yes. A frustrated romance was better than nothing. You had to assert yourself sort of . . . sexually. You know what I mean?'

Charles nodded. 'Yes. Have a sexual identity. At best a lover, at worst an idol.' He played his bait out gently. 'A public figure, maybe . . . A symbol . . . Perhaps just a poster . . .'

Pam flushed suddenly and he knew he had a bite. 'I found the poster torn up in the dustbin.'

'Ah.' She looked down shamefaced.

'Did you love Willy Mariello?'

'No. It was just . . . I don't know. All this pressure, and then Puce came to play at the Union and I met him. And, you know, he was a rock star . . .'

'Potent symbol.'

'Yes. And lots of the other girls in the hall of residence thought he was marvellous and bought posters and . . .' She looked up defiantly. 'It's terrible emotional immaturity, I know. But I am emotionally immature. Thanks to a middle-class upbringing. It was just a schoolgirl crush.'

'Did you know him well?'

'No, that's what makes it so pathetic. I mean, I knew

82

him to say hello to, but nothing more. He didn't notice me.'

'You never slept with him?'

Her eyes opened wide. 'Oh Lord, no.'

'So why the rush to get rid of the poster?'

'I don't know. That was daft. I was just so confused—what with the death, and the police asking all those questions . . . and then you asking questions . . . I don't know. I got paranoid. I thought somehow if my things were searched and they found the poster that I'd be incriminated or . . . I don't know. I wasn't thinking straight.'

It rang true. The brief mystery of the poster was explained. But there must be more to be found out from Pam. 'What did you feel about Willy when he was dead?'

'Shock. I mean, I hadn't seen a dead body before.'

'Nothing else?'

'No, I don't think so.'

'No sense of loss?'

'Not really. I mean, it wasn't real love, just something I'd built up in my mind. In a way his death got it out of my system, made me realise that I didn't really feel a thing for him. Anyway, it had been fading ever since we came up here.'

'As you saw more of him?'

'Yes.' She grinned ruefully. 'He became more real. Just an ordinary man. And perhaps not a very nice one. Anyway, I didn't really feel the same about him after that business with Lesley . . .'

Charles picked up the last few words as if they were the ash of a vital document in a murderer's fireplace. 'Business with Lesley?'

'Yes, I . . . well, I haven't mentioned it to anyone, but . . . it may be nothing, just the way it seemed . . .'

'What?'

'It was after we'd been up here about a week. Willy suddenly started to take an interest in Lesley—that's Lesley Petter who—'

'I know about her. Go on.'

83

'I think he was probably after her, fancied her, I don't know. Anyway, one evening, after we'd been rehearsing, we were all having coffee back at Coates Gardens and Willy said he was going for a walk up to the Castle and did anyone want to come with him. Well, I said yes sort of straight off, because, you know, I thought he was marvellous and . . . But then I realised that he'd only said that as a sort of pre-arranged signal to Lesley. It was meant to be just the two of them.

'I was awfully embarrassed, but I couldn't say I wouldn't go when I realised. So the three of us set off and I dawdled or went ahead or . . . wishing like anything I wasn't there.

'We went up to the Castle Esplanade and wandered around, and I, feeling more and more of a gooseberry, went on ahead on the way back. I started off down the steps that go down to Johnstone Terrace.'

'Castle Wynd South.'

'Is that what it's called, yes. Anyway, I was nearly at the bottom, and suddenly I heard this scream. I turned round and saw Lesley, with her arms and legs flailing, falling down the steps.'

'And that was how she broke her leg?'

'Yes. I rushed up to where she'd managed to stop herself, and Willy rushed down. She was in terrible pain and I shot off to phone for an ambulance. But just before I went, I heard her say something to Willy, or at least I think I did.'

Charles felt the excitement prickling over his shoulders and neck. 'What did she say?'

'She said, "Willy, you pushed me." '

CHAPTER SEVEN

"Be thou my park, and I will be thy dear,"
(So he began at least to speak or quote;)
"Be thou my bark, and I thy gondolier,"
(For passion takes this figurative note;)
"Be thou my light, and I thy chandelier;
Be thou my dove, and I will be thy cote;
My lily be, and I will be thy river;
Be thou my life—and I will be thy liver."

BIANCA'S DREAM

THE SHOW BIZ RAZZMATAZZ of first nights was invented before the development of lunchtime theatre. There is something incongruous about flowers and telegrams for a first lunch. Charles did not get any, anyway. There was no one to send them. Maurice Skellern was the only person outside Edinburgh who knew the show was happening and he was not the sort to spend his client's money on fulsome gestures. Charles deliberately had not told his ex-wife Frances that he was going up to the Festival as another hack at the fraying but resilient umbilical cord that joined him to her.

But the first night excitement was there. He walked from Coates Gardens to the Masonic Hall with a jumpy step, a little gurgling void of anticipation in his stomach. To his relief, the odious Plug had been replaced by an amiable young man called Vernon, who was not only efficient in the rehearsal but was also staying for the show. It made Charles feel more confident. And more scared. With the technical side under control, no excuses were possible; it was his responsibility entirely.

He calmed himself by hard work. One run of the show for Vernon's benefit, to get the cues right; then a quick double-check through all the slides; finally an as-per-performance run which was depressingly pedestrian. As it should be. Charles believed in the old theatrical adage about bad dress rehearsals leading to good first nights.

A few more details checked, then down to the pub about twelve-thirty for a quick one. Just one; mustn't risk slurring. Vernon was quiet and reassuring, a good companion for last-minute anxieties. Yes, he would hold the last fade. Yes, he would anticipate the slide of *The Last Man* sitting on the gallows. No, he didn't think there was too much serious stuff in the programme. No, he didn't think the dark suit was too anonymous.

Back at the hall Brian Cassells was in charge as Front of House Manager. Apparently he felt that evening dress was obligatory for this rôle, though he looked a little out of place penguined up at lunchtime. He admitted to Charles that advance sales were not that good (three seats), but he had great hopes for casual trade during the next twenty minutes.

Sharp on one fifteen the show started. Charles had felt on the edge of nausea as he waited to enter in the blackout, but as usual actually being onstage gave him a sense of calm and control.

The imperfect masking of the hall's windows meant that the audience was visible, but he did not dare to look until he had received some reaction. The watershed was *Faithless Nellie Gray*; nothing expected on *I Remember, I Remember* and the rest of the preamble. But the first Pathetic Ballad should get something.

> Ben Battle was a soldier bold,
>   And used to war's alarms;
> But a cannon-ball took off his legs,
>   So he laid down his arms.

Yes, a distinct laugh. And the laughs built through the ensuing stanzas. Not a big sound, but warming.

Emboldened, he inspected the audience as he recited. About twenty, which, on the first day of the Festival, with

86

negative publicity, was not bad. On a second glance he realised that a lot of it was paper, members of D.U.D.S. who had been allowed in free. There was a little knot of revue cast, dark figures grouped around Anna's shining head. James Milne leant forward in his seat with intense concentration. There were only about eight faces Charles did not recognise. And some of those might be complimentaries for the critics. Maurice Skellern was not going to be over-impressed by ten per cent of fifty per cent of that lot.

But it was an audience. And they were responding. Charles enjoyed himself.

The Laird insisted on taking him out to lunch. They went to an Indian restaurant on Forrest Place and managed to persuade the waiter it was still early enough for them to have a bottle of wine. After a couple of glasses Charles felt better. The immediate reaction after a show was always emptiness, even depression, and the ability to remember only the things that went wrong. Gradually it passed; alcohol always speeded the process.

So did enthusiastic response to the show. And James Milne was very enthusiastic. He had only known the familiar poems of Hood, the ones which have become clichés by repetition, *No-vember*, *A Retrospective Review*, *The Song of the Shirt* and the inevitable *I Remember, I Remember*. The broadening of the picture which Charles's show had given obviously excited him. The punning and other verbal tricks appealed to his crossword mind. 'I had no idea there was so much variety, Charles. I really must get hold of a *Complete Works*. Is there a good edition?'

'There's an Oxford one, but I don't know if it's in print. You might be able to pick up a second-hand one somewhere. Or there are some fairly good selections. But look, if you want to borrow mine, do. I should know my words by now.' He held the copy across the table.

The Laird was touched. By his values, lending a book was

the highest form of friendship. 'That's very kind. I'll look after it.'

'I know you will.'

'And I'll make it a priority to find one for myself. Oh, you know I envy that kind of facility with words. Not just the facility—we all happen on puns occasionally—but the ability to create something out of it. It must be wonderful to be a writer.'

'I don't know. It was hard graft for Hood. If he hadn't had to work so hard, he might have lived longer.'

'Yes, but at least it's congenial graft. I mean, writing, you're on your own, you get on with it, you don't have to keep getting involved with other people. You just write and send your stuff off and that's it. A sort of remote control way of making a living.'

Charles laughed out loud. 'James, you've got it all wrong. Hood would disagree with you totally. He didn't just sit at a desk toying with his muse and packing the products off in envelopes to editors. All his life was spent scurrying round, selling his own work, sub-editing other people's, setting up magazines. No question of remote control, his Liveli-Hood, as he kept calling it, was very much involved with other people.'

'But some writers don't have to do all that, Charles.'

'Very few. In my own experience of writing plays, about ten per cent of the time is spent actually writing; ninety per cent is traipsing round like a peddler, hawking the results to managements or television companies.'

'Oh dear. So what you are saying is that a writer's life is just as sordid and ordinary as everyone else's?'

'If not more so. Hood himself, in his *Copyright and Copywrong*, said of writers, "We are on a par with quack doctors, street preachers, strollers, ballad-singers, hawkers of last dying speeches, Punch and Judies, conjurers, tumblers and other diverting vagabonds." '

'How very disappointing. I think I'd rather forget you

told me that and keep my illusions of ivory towers and groves of Academe.'

They talked further about writing. James Milne admitted that he would have liked to produce something himself, but never got around to it. 'Which means perhaps that I haven't really got anything to say.'

'Maybe. Though writing doesn't have to say anything. It can just be there to entertain,' said Charles, reflecting on his own few plays.

'Hmm. Perhaps, but even then the writer must get a bit involved. Begin to identify with his characters.'

'Oh, inevitably that happens.'

The Laird paused for a moment, piecing his thoughts together. 'I was wondering if there could be anything of that behind this murder.'

'What do you mean? Anything of what?'

'Identification. I mean, if there's anything in the actual situation of the killing, the way it happened.'

'I'm still not with you.'

'Willy Mariello was playing David Rizzio in a play based on the life of Mary, Queen of Scots. Now there are certain obvious parallels between Willy and Rizzio. There's the Italian name, for a start. I know there are lots of Scots with Italian names, but it's a coincidence. Then they both played the guitar.'

'So what you're suggesting,' Charles said slowly, 'is that someone got obsessed with the whole Mary, Queen of Scots story and identified with Rizzio's murder and ... Incidentally, who did kill Rizzio?'

'A lot of people, I seem to recall. I think Darnley was the prime mover. Who's playing Darnley in the show?'

'I don't know. I could check. And you think when we've got that name we've got our murderer?' He could not keep a note of scepticism out of his voice.

'It's just another possible line of enquiry. Something that struck me.'

'Hmm.'

'Well, we're not getting far on any other tack, are we?'
Charles hesitated. 'No.'

'You haven't found out anything else, have you?'

'No,' he lied. For some reason he did not want to tell anyone about Pam Northcliffe's story of Willy and Lesley. Not yet.

The Laird was going to browse round some bookshops, but Charles did not feel like it. He was still wound up after the performance, and, since licensing hours did not permit his usual method of unwinding, he decided an aimless stroll round Edinburgh might do the trick.

The stroll soon ceased to be aimless. He had only gone a few hundred yards and was turning off George IV bridge into Chambers Street when he saw Martin Warburton. Striding along on the opposite side of the road with the same expression of blinkered concentration that he had had the day before. And again heading for Nicholson Street.

It is a lot easier following someone when you know where he is going and Charles felt confident of Martin's destination. He was right. The boy again disappeared behind the blue door.

The excitement of seeing the same thing happen two days running quickly gave way to confusion as to what should be done about it. Charles still did not know which flat Martin had gone into and did not feel in the mood for an elaborate masquerade as a reader of gas-meters to gain access. Apart from the risk of illegal impersonation, what would he say if he did find Martin? There was probably some simple explanation for the boy's actions. He had friends living in the flats. Maybe even a girl-friend. Something quite straight-forward. Charles was just letting his imagination run riot and suspicion was clouding his judgement.

But he did not want to go. He might be on the verge of some discovery. Better join the bus queue opposite while he worked out a plan of campaign.

As he stood with the laden housewives and noisy schoolchildren he knew it was not really getting him anywhere. No plan of campaign emerged. If he really wanted to find out what Martin was doing, then the only course was to enter the flats. Otherwise he might just as well give up the whole business, leave Willy Mariello to the police and forget any detective fantasies he might be nurturing.

A bus arrived and the queue surged forward, canny housewives wedging themselves into good seats and practised schoolchildren scampering upstairs to good fooling-about positions. One or two of them gave curious looks to the man at the stop who still queued altruistically without taking his due prize of a seat. The maroon and white bus passed on.

Charles felt exposed and ridiculous on his own at the bus-stop. He turned to go, determined to chuck the whole business and resign himself to just being an actor, when he heard the bang of a door on the other side of the road.

It was the blue one, and a thin figure was walking away from it towards the centre of the city. Walking with a determined gait, but not walking like Martin Warburton. It was a slightly unnatural heavier step.

And not looking like Martin Warburton either. A woollen hat gave the impression of short hair. A beard and moustache. Glasses. Dressed in an old donkey jacket and shapeless twill trousers. A khaki knapsack slung across one shoulder. And this strange ponderous walk.

It was the figure whom Charles had seen the previous week on the steps down to the Mound. And it was Martin Warburton in disguise.

By eleven o'clock that evening Martin's identity games did not seem very important. One reason was that the afternoon's adventures had not led to anything. Charles had continued tailing his disguised quarry half-way across Edinburgh until Martin had disappeared inside the Scottish National Portrait Gallery in Queen Street. Rather than risk raising suspicions by a confrontation inside the building, the self-questioning sleuth had waited twenty minutes some way down the road.

91

Then he had followed the donkey jacket back to Nicholson Street, missed a few more buses while the young man was reconverted into Martin Warburton and trailed behind that familiar figure back to Coates Gardens. All of which left Charles with sore feet and the feeling that if Martin wanted to do his Edinburgh sightseeing in disguise, that was his own affair. And that Charles Paris needed a drink.

Which accounted for the other reason why Martin's behaviour seemed unimportant. Charles was satisfyingly pissed.

After solitary refuelling at the pub, he had found Anna with the rest of the revue team at Coates Gardens. He had taken her out for a meal, to celebrate the opening of his show and keep her mind off the opening of hers. They went to the Casa Española in Rose Street and, since Anna was in a high state of nerves, he had to eat most of a large paella and drink all of the wine. A fate which he embraced with fortitude and which contributed to his present well-being.

It had also been encouraging to see Anna nervous. She was as jumpy as a kitten and it was the first time he had seen her lose her cool at all. Which made her seem more human. And even nicer.

Charles thought of her warmly as he sat in the Masonic Hall and fingered her key in his pocket. He had the drunkard's feeling of sexual omnicompetence and longed to be with her in the bed over the Lawnmarket. It would not be long. After the revue. He would go discreetly back to the flat and then, after the company giggles and congratulations, she would join him.

The lights dimmed. Not bad; the house was two-thirds full. He sat back in the right mood to enjoy *Brown Derby*— 'Simply the Funniest Late-Night Revue on the Fringe.'

If it was, it did not say a lot for the others. *Brown Derby* was a hotch-potch of styles. Decrepit jokes that should have been allowed quiet deaths were resuscitated and paraded as new. Dull irrelevant puns were presented as wit. The ill-digested influence of television comedy made for uncomfortable production. Though there were flashes of humour, the show was heavy going, and never heavier than in its topical material. The comments on the British political scene showed neither insight nor understanding and the piece on the American presidency was frankly embarrassing. Ten days after President Nixon's resignation was not the time for a naïve and tasteless parody of Adolf Hitler in his bunker (including some pretty tired jokes about golf).

And it was not a case of a brilliant new team struggling valiantly against unworthy material. The cast was not good. If acting at its most basic is making oneself heard and not bumping into the furniture, they failed as actors on two counts. They were rarely audible and kept tripping over chairs (especially during the extended blackouts between sketches, with the result that the lights usually came up on some puzzled youth lying full length on the upturned furniture). They had almost no talent.

Except for Anna. She was extraordinarily good and, given the lack of competition, dominated the show completely. Singing, dancing, flashing through a variety of accents and costumes, she was the only person onstage with any concept of pace or comedy. The direness of the material she had to perform only highlighted her skill.

Charles was amazed. Anna was a beautiful girl, but onstage she was animated by an extra charge that intensified her beauty. A real stage presence. He could feel the men in the audience responding to her. When she came on for her last number *A Bunny Girl's Lament* (a reasonable idea, marred by flabby lyrics), dressed in full Playboy Club kit, showing her long brown legs, the audience broke into spontaneous applause. It was not just that she looked sexy; she managed to incorporate an archness which distanced her from her material and was also extremely funny. Anna Duncan was that rare creature, a woman who can be funny onstage without sacrificing either her dignity or her sex appeal.

*　　*　　*

93

It was late when she tapped on the door of the Lawn-market flat. The first night junketings must have gone on a bit. Perhaps the *Brown Derby* cast had been drowning their sorrows. Or perhaps they were celebrating, thinking that the enthusiastic final applause for Anna was meant for all of them.

She looked him straight in the eye. 'Well, what's your cool professional assessment?'

'Can you take it?'

'Yes.'

'Well, I'm afraid I thought the show was terrible. The only constructive suggestions that I can make are that your writers should go and sell vacuum cleaners, your male cast should join the Army and your director should become a monk.'

'Hmm.' The navy blue eyes kept their level gaze fixed on him. She knew there was more to come.

So he let it come. 'I would also like to say that you are one of the most talented young actresses I have ever seen.'

She smiled and allowed herself a slight relaxation of relief. 'Charles, I asked for your cool professional assessment.'

'That was my cool professional assessment.'

'Hmm. Sounds biased.' But she was obviously delighted.

'Biased nothing! I may also happen to think you are the best screw in the world, but I do genuinely believe that you are exceptionally talented as an actress. Now come and make love.'

She grinned suddenly. 'You talked me into it.'

It was even better. They were completely together. He rolled apart from her and cradled the strong slender body in his arms. Her breasts were slack against his ribs, her breath soft on his shoulder. He recited gently into her hair.

' "O, happy times! O happy rhymes!

   For ever ye're gone by!

Few now—if any—are the lays

   Can make me smile or sigh." But you're one of them. You can make me smile and sigh.'

'I don't think Thomas Hood meant "lay" that way,' she murmured lazily.

'No, I don't think he did.'

'Incidentally, I liked your show. I think I was too uptight over dinner to mention it.'

'Thank you. Mutual admiration society.'

'Hmm.' There was a long pause. He wondered if she had gone to sleep. But she spoke again. 'Do you really think I'm good?'

'Yes.'

'Good enough to make it in the professional theatre?'

'Yes.'

'In spite of all you said about needing to be tough and calculating, and needing lots of help?'

'I'll help you, Anna.'

Soon she was asleep. Charles lay thinking. He could help her. Get her work, maybe. Even cast her in plays he was directing. He felt useful and wanted to give to her. To give a lot. Was it so ridiculous for a man of nearly forty-eight to go round with a girl in her early twenties? His experience could help her. He felt something for Anna that he had not felt for a long, long time. Possibly even love.

CHAPTER EIGHT

O William Dear! O William Dear!
My rest eternal ceases;
Alas! my everlasting peace
Is broken into pieces.
MARY'S GHOST

TUESDAY 20TH AUGUST was an unsettling day.

It started all right. Charles felt at one with Anna and at one with the world. She left the flat at about half-past nine. (Michael Vanderzee was champing at the bit to get his workshop sessions restarted after the lay-off caused by the revue's opening.) Charles had a leisurely breakfast of floury bacon rolls at the Poppin and then, as a token gesture to detective work, he went back to the Scottish National Portrait Gallery to see if he could work out the reason for Martin's visit.

The Gallery was well laid out and should have been interesting, but he was not in the mood for inspecting the faces of people he had never heard of. The whole business of searching for clues and motives was beginning to bore him.

He was gazing at a wax model of William III when he remembered the newspapers. The day after a first night (or at least a first lunch) and he had not yet checked to see if there were any notices. The rest of the portraits could wait. He hurried out under the disapproving glare of the large-nosed faces of Scotland's heritage.

There was a big newsagents on Princes Street. Rather than behaving logically and starting with just the *Guardian,* he went mad and bought every available daily. Which meant a great deal of waste paper; *So Much Comic* ... had so far failed to capture the interest of the nationals.

He stood in the street reading and dropped the inadequate newspapers one by one into a litter-bin. Nothing in the *Guardian*; so much for his conversation at the Fringe Reception. Charles realised he was being naïvely optimistic to expect to be noticed on the first day of the Festival, particularly with negative advertising.

Only the *Glasgow Herald* left. He opened it without hope, and on the review page, there it was.

So Much Comic, So Much Blood, Masonic Hall, Lauriston Place. Thomas Hood is now remembered, if at all, for about three poems which recur in anthologies. It was therefore a pleasant surprise to get a broader view of the poet's work from this enchanting lunch-time show. Charles Paris has compiled a skilful programme from poems and letters, which maintains a fine balance between humour and pathos without ever slipping into sentimentality. He performs the show with the clarity and understatement which are the hallmark of real talent. Do try to catch this. It's only on for the first week of the Festival and I guarantee more laughs than in most of the late-night revues.

Charles could not control an ebullient smile. What he held in his hands was a good old-fashioned rave.

Thanks to the review and a couple of large Bell's, he arrived at the Masonic Hall at a quarter to one in high spirits and totally devoid of nerves. He felt confident as he waited in the wings for the lights to go down.

From that point on the day deteriorated. For a start, the show did not go well. A second performance is always difficult, because of the feeling of anticlimax. And the size of the audience did not augur well for the circulation figures of the *Glasgow Herald*. There were about twenty, apparently under doctor's orders that laughter was injurious to health.

Puns and wisecracks vanished into the spongy void of the hall.

And, to add to that, Frances was in the audience. The woman he had married, to whom he had given the unfortunate name of Frances Paris. He recognised her as soon as the show started from her loyal, and solitary, laughter. When he stopped to consider, it was quite logical that she should be in Edinburgh. She came up most summers to give a couple of her sixth formers a quick cultural immersion. There were two girls sitting with her, one black and one white.

Charles was very fond of Frances, but he wished she was not there. Since he had walked out on her twelve years before, they had remained friendly and he had even gone back to her from time to time. She made no demands on him, but her presence, just when he was feeling secure of his relationship with Anna, was embarrassing.

He tried not to be too off-hand when she came round backstage; he had no desire to hurt her. She looked harassed and was obviously having difficulty controlling her two charges outside the school context. The white girl was dumpy and called Candy; the black girl was splendidly tangible and called Jane; both regarded Edinburgh as an opportunity to be emancipated and *meet men*.

Husband and wife exchanged Edinburgh addresses and parted amicably with vague intentions to meet up again. The encounter brought a little cloud of depression into Charles's sunny outlook.

It was not until about half past six that the cloud started to look stormy. The *Mary* cast had been rehearsing all afternoon, but most of them were released for the evening, because Michael Vanderzee wanted to work on the Mary/Bothwell scenes for an hour until Anna had to go to the revue. After a cabbage supper at Coates Gardens, the actor playing John Knox (nicknamed 'Opportunity Knox' by the rest of the cast) suggested a trip to the pub. Darnley, Ruthven and Cardinal Beaton thought it was a good idea.

So did the new David Rizzio, Sam Wasserman. Charles decided that he too would like a drink.

In the Haymarket pub, he discovered that student unrest manifests itself in reluctance to be first to the bar, so he bought the round. Without conscious engineering, he found himself alone at a table with Sam.

The author of *Mary, Queen of Sots* was a young American with fine blond hair, a woffly ginger moustache and black-rimmed round glasses. He wore a thick check lumberjack shirt, the inevitable blue jeans and yellow-laced brown boots. He had arrived in Edinburgh that day, just in time to hear the boom of the one o'clock gun fired from the Castle and become immediately embroiled in one of Michael Vanderzee's workshops.

'That was after two solid days' travelling. I got Mike's telegram from the Poste Restante in Brindisi, and I just dropped everything and came. I mean, my God. I really care about this show . . .'

As soon as Sam started speaking, Charles realised why the tête-à-tête had been so easily arranged. Sam Wasserman was a bore, one of those instantly identifiable bores who has the ability to make the most interesting anecdote tedious, who can destroy by endless detail. But as well as qualifying as one of this international type, Sam also demonstrated that refinement of the quality which is peculiar to earnest young American academics. A glaze crept over Charles' eyes as the monologue continued.

'. . . . In fact, *Mary, Queen of Sots* derives directly from the presentation techniques I developed in a show based on the Boston Tea Party for my Master's thesis at U.S.C. . . .'

'U.S.C.?' Charles queried weakly.

'University of Southern California. I did my Master's there before coming to Derby. In Drama and Creative Writing. When I say my project was based on the Boston Tea Party, I mean of course loosely based. It concentrated on the ethnico-political problems of the American Indians. Viewed of course from a Socialist standpoint. The central allegorical symbol was the fact that the Boston Tea Party was perpetrated by white men disguised as Indians. White usurping the place of red. Like corpuscles. I used the analogy of leukemia.'

Charles concentrated and tried to nudge the conversation in the direction he wanted. 'But you come to this show in rather macabre circumstances.'

The nudge was insufficient; Sam needed actual derailment. 'The macabre is very much an integral part of my writing. And the bizarre. Another image I developed in the U.S.C. show,' he steamrollered on, 'was the unusual ability of the Navajo Indians to walk along girders at great height as if they were on the ground. It's a different spatial concept. I related that to the myopic nature of the social services . . .'

'Oh.' Charles found himself nodding like a toy dog in the back of a car. He made another supreme effort to manhandle Sam off his monologue. 'What I meant was that Willy Mariello was killed with a knife and that's why you're here actually taking part in *Mary, Queen of Sots.*'

For a moment it seemed to have worked. Sam looked straight at him and was silent for a long time before his continuation showed that Charles had failed. 'Well, of course, *Mary* is an entirely different proposition, in spite of certain similarities of technique. And in fact, from an allegorical point of view, it's very apt that the show should be born in an atmosphere of violence.

'You see, the basic allegory of *Mary, Queen of Sots* is the historical parallel. The original Mary's life was stained with blood. In my version, Mary, Queen of Scots represents Scotland and the natural wealth of her oil resources.'

'Oh yes,' Charles mouthed, wilting.

'Yes,' said Sam, as if it were a surprising affirmation. 'Now Mary's two husbands, Lord Darnley and the Earl of Bothwell, I take to represent England and the good old U.S. of A., the two countries who want to control her wealth. Queen Elizabeth, who ordains her execution, is the

Arab states, who hold the real power in oil politics. Neat, huh?'

Charles, suffering from mental indigestion at the thought of this laboured allegory being expounded in Creative Writing, nodded feebly. But he saw a slight chance. 'Where does David Rizzio fit into this scenario?'

'David Rizzio represents the ecological lobby who might argue against the exploitation of oil resources in favour of a more medieval economic structure. For that reason, he gets killed off pretty early.' Sam chuckled at his own intellectual audacity.

It might be a tiny lever to shift the conversation and Charles seized it. 'But not killed off as early as Willy Mariello was.'

'No.'

Before Sam had time to relate the death to one of his allegories, Charles pressed on. 'You must have been pretty cut up to hear about Willy.'

'Shocked certainly. I mean one is always shocked to hear of a young person's death; it's a kind of suspension of continuity. And obviously there was a dramatic element in this particular event.'

'But you must have felt this more. To lose a friend . . .'

'I didn't know Mariello that well.'

'I thought it was through you that Willy came to be in this show in the first place.'

'That's true, but only indirectly. I suppose the suggestion that he should do the music came from me—I put it up to the D.U.D.S. committee—but that was on the recommendation of someone else.'

'Who?'

'A girl involved in the society suggested it. I thought it was a good idea, because, you know, he was a professional musician and into rock music and I, well, I've got a kind of basic musical knowledge, but really my talent lies with *words*. And certainly the settings Mariello did for my lyrics were infinitely superior to anything I could have done. He changed the odd word here and there and I had to pull him up on that, but basically it was great. Besides, I believe very strongly in people working together under a kind of creative umbrella unit'.

'Why do you think the girl recommended Willy to you?' Charles asked slowly.

'Well, like I say, he was very good. And he'd been hanging round the Derby campus for a bit and apparently, after the group he was with split up, he wanted to try something different . . .'

'And?'

'Well, I kind of got the impression that there might be a kind of thing going on between him and this girl. They both played it pretty close to the chest, but I sort of got this feeling that they wouldn't mind being involved in something together.'

'Oh,' said Charles, and then asked the question he had been putting off. 'Who was this girl?'

'A girl called Anna Duncan. She's now playing Mary in my show. I don't know if you know her.'

'Oh yes,' said Charles, 'I know her.'

That evening he met James Milne back at Coates Gardens and found the Laird eager for another Dr Watson session. Charles had suddenly become unwilling to pursue the business of detection, but he could not avoid a cosy chat over malt whisky.

Sherlock Holmes was always way ahead of Dr Watson in his deductions, but he rarely actually withheld information from his sidekick. Charles Paris did. There were things he wanted to be sure of, half-formed ideas that could not be shared until they had hardened into facts.

They talked mostly about Martin Warburton. Charles told of his long tracking expeditions and the discovery of Martin's second identity.

'But surely that makes him our number one suspect?'

'I suppose so.' Charles hoped he sounded convinced.

'It's fairly bizarre behaviour.'

'Yes, I agree. Certainly Martin is in a very strange mental state. He's all mixed up and he has some violent fantasies. I think he's probably suffering from overwork—you know, just taken finals—but that doesn't make him a murderer. His disguise may be for criminal purposes, or it may just be that he needs to escape into another identity.'

'Hmm. That sounds like psychological claptrap to me.'

'You don't subscribe to a psychological approach to crime?'

'I dare say it's very useful in certain cases, but I think it's often used to fog perfectly straightforward issues. Every action has some sort of motive, and I'm sure that Martin Warburton has a real motive for dressing up as someone else.'

'And you don't regard an inadequacy in his personality as a real motive?'

'I regard it as a formula of words. A motive is theft or blackmail, that sort of thing. Revenge even.'

'But Martin might take on another identity because there's something in his own that he can't come to terms with.'

'I don't really know what you're talking about.'

It was so easy for the Laird, insulated from life in his library, just as he had been insulated with his mother at Glenloan House and insulated in the staffroom at Kilbruce School. Because he had never encountered any unpleasant realities, he assumed they did not exist. Or if they did, they were simple things that could be cut up like sheets of paper, not made of material that frayed and tore and could never be properly divided.

'But, James, come off it. When we last spoke you were talking of an obsessional killer, someone for whom the Mary, Queen of Scots story had a macabre significance.'

'I didn't quite say that.'

'You were moving in that direction. And an obsessional killer hasn't got one of your nice neatly defined motives like theft or blackmail or revenge.'

'Yes, he has. The very obsession is the motive. It's not a sane motive, but it's real to the murderer.'

'Therefore you've got to understand the psychology of the murderer.' Charles felt that it was a mild triumph.

'Yes, but the process is simple. Assume an inverted logic, and the motivation makes sense. You don't have to delve into inadequacies of personality and compensation and all that humbug.'

'I don't think we're going to agree on this point.' Charles was beginning to lose the little interest he had in their discussion. His mind was elsewhere, and not enjoying the trip. But he felt he should simulate some concern. 'So if Martin, say, is an obsessional killer, what do you reckon is the motive for his walking round the city of Edinburgh in disguise?'

'It must be something to do with the planning of his next crime.'

'I see.' Charles tried not to sound contemptuous. 'So what do you think we should do about it?'

'I think we should keep a close eye on him.'

'Yes, fine. I must go.' He rose with almost rude abruptness. 'I've got to . . . um . . . go.' He could not think of a polite excuse. He could not think of anything except the ordeal ahead of him. The ordeal of seeing Anna.

When it came, it was not really an ordeal. She arrived, flushed and excited after the revue. There had been a B.B.C. producer in the audience who (according to Brian Cassells, who had buttonholed the poor man departing and forced an opinion out of him) had liked Anna's performance. She was very giggly and charming as she described Brian's earnest relaying of the news and imagined his clumsy handling of the encounter. Charles warmed to her in spite of himself.

But he felt detached because of the tiny infection of suspicion inside him. He kept wanting to ask her about Willy, to know if they had had an affair and, by doing so, cauterise the wound before it spread to dangerous proportions. But he could not do it. Not when she was so lovely. It would spoil everything.

They drank some port that Anna had bought and giggled into bed. And they made love. As good as ever, tender, synchronised, good. Except that Charles felt he was watching the two of them like a picture on the wall. Immediately after, they switched off the light and Anna, who was exhausted by *Mary* rehearsals and the revue, slipped easily into sleep.

Charles did not. He felt better for having seen her; his imagination could not run riot while she was actually there. But the doubt remained. He wanted to excise it, cut it out of his mind. The only way to do that was to ask her point-blank. But he knew he couldn't. Not to her face. He contemplated ringing her up, even ringing her up in a different identity, pretending to be a policeman or . . . No, that was stupid.

He reasoned with himself. All right, so say she had been having an affair with Willy Mariello. So what? Charles had no particular claim on her and, anyway, he never worried about a woman's previous lovers; they didn't concern him. Jealousy over something that was over was pointless. And a lover couldn't be more over than Willy.

That was the worrying bit. Not that Anna had slept with the Scottish lout, but that he had been murdered. Again Charles reasoned with himself and calmed himself with thoughts that there might be no connection between the two facts. Indeed, they weren't both definitive facts yet. And they could be investigated.

Yes, a bit of investigation would put his mind at rest. He plumped up his pillow and turned over. Anna's breathing had a soporific rhythm. But he did not sleep.

CHAPTER NINE

There's some have specs to help their sight
    Of objects dim and small
But Tim had *specks* within his eyes,
    And could not see at all.

TIM TURPIN

T HE FIRST PART of the investigation to set his mind at rest was another call on Jean Mariello.

She opened the door and leaned against it uninvitingly. 'What do you want? There's nothing more I can tell you.'

'Please, just a couple of questions. I think I'm on to something.'

'Big deal. Listen, Mr Paris. I'm very busy packing. The only thing that interests me about Willy is how soon I can forget he ever existed. And I don't want to play cops and robbers.'

'Please give me five minutes.'

'Oh . . .' She hovered between shutting him out and letting him in. Then she drew back. 'Five minutes.' She looked at her watch.

Charles entered the hall and moved into the front room. Jean Mariello gained some of the satisfaction she would have got from slamming the door in his face by slamming it behind him. 'Right. Ask.'

Charles looked round. There were suitcases and cardboard boxes brimful of belongings. In the corner household rubbish and decorating rubble was swept into a neat pile. 'You're going?'

'Yes, the house is on the market. I'll never come back here.'

'You're leaving Edinburgh?'

'Yes. I'm moving in with a man in the folk group. In Newcastle.'

'Won't you miss it?'

'Edinburgh, yes. This house I hope I never see again.'

'It's a nice enough house.'

'Look, I never lived here. Willy only bought the place a few months ago. I've been on tour. The only times I ever saw it, it was covered with paint brushes or plaster dust or other evidence of Willy's latest ideas of home décor. He had the knack of converting every place we lived in into a pigsty. He'd suddenly get sick of his surroundings and want to change it all—smother everything with paint, take down a door . . . and never finish the job. We got turned out of one flat after he decided to take down the partition between the bedroom and sitting-room. Living with Willy was not an experience that gave one a feeling of home. I feel nothing for this place.'

'Oh well, it's in reasonable condition. You should get a good price for it.'

She snorted contemptuously. 'The building society should get a good price for it.'

'Ah. Still, Willy . . .'

She shook her head. 'Willy had no money. He spent everything he made with Puce, not that there was much left after all the agents and managers had taken their bites. There may be a few royalties to come, but they'll go on the bank loan he got for the deposit on this place and the arrears on the mortgage.'

'Arrears?'

'Yes. Willy got the mortgage on the basis of his earnings last year and the assumption that that level of income would continue. Then the band split up and he had virtually nothing. I don't think one single repayment has been made to the building society. Mind you,' she added bitterly, 'I only discover this when he's dead and I have to go through his mail.'

'So you're not exactly a rich widow?'

He got a scornful 'Huh' for that. 'Mr Paris, I can't believe that you came here to talk homes and gardens and mortgages. And if you didn't, your five minutes and my patience are running low.'

'I'm sorry. But just before I ask what I really came for, tell me why Willy bought this house.'

'It fitted the image of what he wanted to be. Saw himself as the great landowner, in his ancestral home in front of his blazing fire. The man of property, Willy, like all social upstarts, couldn't wait to be rich enough to be Conservative. The Socialist pose, the sub-hippy world of rock music—that meant nothing to him really. It was only a stage he had to go through. He wanted to be stinking rich with servants to do everything for him. Trouble was, he was a bloody awful business man and couldn't keep any money for more than five minutes.'

There was a pause. Jean Mariello looked at her watch and Charles realised he could not beat about the bush any longer. 'I really wanted to ask you about Willy's sex life.'

'Oh. Well, of recent years I'm not really an expert on that.'

'No. I wanted to know about another woman.'

'I didn't take a great deal of interest in his other women either.'

Charles ignored the rebuffs and ploughed on. 'When he was in Derby—you know, he stayed after the band had played there—do you know if he had a girl then?'

'I assume so. I can't think he stayed for the scenery.'

'He never mentioned a girl?'

'No. We didn't discuss our private lives.' She glanced at her watch.

'Do you know if he had a girl around recently? You know, in the week before he died?'

She laughed incredulously. 'I wasn't here much of the time. You know that. What do you want me to do—say if I found stains on the sheets or hairs on the pillow?'

'Yes, if necessary.'

That took her aback. She paused and then said in a softer voice. 'All right then, I would say, from the evidence of dirty laundry, that Willy did commit yet another desecration of our marriage bed between the Friday when I left and the Tuesday when he was killed.'

'Yes?'

She spoke slowly, as if unwillingly dredging her memory. 'Oh yes, he'd had someone. Hairs on the pillow, all the old familiar signs.'

'What colour hairs?' asked Charles breathlessly.

'Blonde.' She looked at her watch. 'Five minutes. Good-bye, Mr Paris. We won't meet again.'

The audience for *So Much Comic, So Much Blood* was larger and they saw a competent performance by Charles Paris. There were some laughs, although the show had no more animation than a slot-machine. As Charles' voice wove its way through Hood's tortuous puns, his mind was elsewhere.

After the show, he gathered his possessions together for a quick exit. There was something important that had to be done before three o'clock.

The women's wards in the Royal Infirmary off Lauriston Place are much the same as in other hospitals. The one Charles entered had the usual mixture of patients. An old lady stared ahead with liquid blue eyes, her long white hair radiating over the pillows. A plump bed-ridden blonde chattered to a morose husband. A homely housewife's face still registered surprise at being hospitalised and half-listened to the sympathy of a lady in a hat. Screens hid one bed and prompted unhealthy thoughts. A thin, thin woman with shiny skin lay as still as her pillow. And, in the corner bed, was a young girl with her plastered left leg raised on a pulley.

Visiting ended in ten minutes; no time to waste. 'Hello. Are you Lesley Petter?'

The girl looked up and acknowledged that she was. Brown hair, shrewd brown eyes, well-proportioned but unremarkable features. Hers was the sort of face that needed emotion to animate it; in repose it was ordinary.

Charles' approach had brought some light into her eyes. Anything was more interesting than the pile of magazines, thrillers and ragged-edged French novels.

'I'm Charles Paris.'

'Oh. You've taken over my lunchtime show.'

'Yes. It's an ill wind.'

She laughed wryly. 'How's it going?'

'O.K.'

'It's about Thomas Hood, isn't it?'

'Yes.' He did not want to elaborate, though the girl's intelligent eyes indicated sensible opinions on the subject. 'I'm really here for a purpose.'

'Of course.' She was disappointed, but philosophical. 'Though I can't think what purpose of yours could involve me.'

'No. Maybe it doesn't involve you.' He tried to think of a way to phrase his questions. 'I . . . there's . . . I don't know, your group . . . D.U.D.S., there's something strange going on there.'

'It must seem strange to an outsider coming in.'

'No, I expect that, as a middle-aged man with a bunch of whizz-kids. I mean strange in . . . well, there's Willy Mariello's death.'

A shutter of caution flicked across her eyes. 'Yes. That was terrible.'

'And, of course, your accident.'

'Yes.' She seemed anxious to move the dialogue into a more flippant direction. 'Somebody must have whistled in the dressing-room or quoted Macbeth or had real flowers onstage or broken another of the show business taboos.'

Charles laughed. He was also relieved at the postponement of his questions. 'You know it all. Do you want to go into the theatre?'

'Yes, I did. But . . . I don't know how good I am as an actress. Oh, I'd done bits all right, but the thing I'm really good at is dancing.' She looked down the bed at the grotesque suspended limb.

'It'll heal all right.'

She patently did not believe his diagnosis, though she said 'Oh yes' as if there were no question.

Charles retreated to safer ground. 'Anyway, I'm sure you must be a good actress. I mean, you were playing Mary and doing the revue and . . .'

'I got the parts, yes. I don't know how I'd have done them, whether I'd have got good press or . . .'

'Well . . .' He could not think of anything suitable.

'Anna got a very good notice for the revue.' It was just a statement, without malice or jealousy.

'Yes, I gather she did.' Charles instinctively and defensively made it sound as if he hardly knew who was being referred to.

'And I think she'll be better than I would have been in *Mary*.'

'Who knows.' He found himself blushing. 'As I said, it's an ill wind.'

'Yes.'

There was a slight pause. A bell sounded, muffled, from an adjacent ward and he blurted out his question. 'Lesley, did Willy Mariello push you down those steps?'

She looked at him in amazement and opened her mouth to reply. But she swallowed the instinctive answer and said in a controlled voice, 'No. No. Why should he?'

It was too controlled. Charles was not convinced. 'Are you sure he didn't? I heard a rumour to the contrary.'

'People shouldn't spread rumours,' she said sharply. There was confusion in her face. 'Listen, Willy's dead. My leg's broken, there's nothing can be done about that. Does it matter?'

'Yes, it does.'

'Well, I don't know. To be quite honest I don't.' She was floundering, an essentially nice girl unable to come to terms with something unpalatable. 'I was confused when it happened and I suppose I turned on the nearest person. I . . I don't know. I mean, would Willy do something like that? What had he possibly got to gain from doing it?'

Charles restricted himself to answering the first question. 'Willy was capable of that sort of thing; he was a lout.'

She looked shocked at this speaking ill of the dead. A bell was rung loudly in the corridor outside the ward. There was a rustle of parcels and final messages from the other visitors. Lesley looked at Charles pleadingly. 'If he did it, I'm sure it was only high spirits, or horseplay or . . .'

'You mean he did do it?'

'I don't know. I . . .'

'Did he push you?'

'Yes, he did.'

Charles left her with assurances that he would try to visit again. And he meant to. Poor kid, stuck in hospital in a strange city where all her friends were too busy to remember her.

The brown eyes were troubled when he left. And it was not just loneliness. She had managed to convince herself since the accident that it really had been a mistake, an unfortunate overflow of youthful exuberance. Now she had been forced to destroy that illusion and her kind nature was finding it difficult to believe that anyone could be so evil.

Charles had no difficulty in believing it. To him the human capacity for evil suddenly seemed infinite.

CHAPTER TEN

Thus Pleasure oft eludes our grasp
Just when we think to grip her;
And hunting after Happiness,
We only hunt a slipper.
                    THE EPPING HUNT

Two things were clear. One, a confrontation with Anna was now unavoidable. And two, he could not face that confrontation himself. He still treasured a hope that everything would be all right, that there was an innocent explanation for the disturbing chain of events that his logic was joining up. And, if his suspicions proved unfounded, he did not want to let them blight his budding relationship with the girl. There was too much at risk. She was the first woman to touch his emotions for years.

He considered the possibilities of disguise, but rejected them. As an actor, he was capable of convincing physical transformations, and he had used disguise before to gain information. But then he had not been trying to hide his identity from people he knew; here he would be trying to fool a girl he had been sleeping with. No disguise would work at close quarters under those circumstances. Even the varied wardrobe of Edinburgh's many old clothes shops and the wizardry of film make-up with foam rubber padding, latex masks and coloured contact lenses would not stand close scrutiny.

He regretted that he could not use the excitement of dressing up to take his mind off the depressing tracks it was moving along. And, like most actors, he found it easier to perform difficult tasks in character than as himself. He visualised appearing to Anna in a total disguise, confirming her innocence by a few well-placed questions, then unmasking and making a joke of it.

But it was just a fantasy. He was being influenced by Martin Warburton and the strong attraction of channelling unpleasant parts of himself into another identity. The fact remained that dressing up would not work.

He contemplated interrogation by telephone. A disembodied voice could be convincingly disguised. But that introduced the problem of an identity. Who would Anna be likely to give information to in a telephone conversation? There were only two answers—someone she knew or a policeman. The first was out and Charles did not feel inclined to risk the second. On a previous occasion he had had it pointed out to him that impersonation of a policeman is a serious offence. And if Anna did have something criminal to hide, the last person she would tell about it was an investigating officer of the law. What was needed was an interrogator who had some other justifiable reason for meeting her and who could introduce relevant questions into the conversation with some pretence at casual enquiry.

Which meant an accomplice. It was Wednesday. Gerald Venables should be back from his weekend in Cannes. Charles rang his Grosvenor Street office from a call-box in the Royal Mile.

Gerald was back. 'How's the sleuth-work going, Charles?'

'I don't know really. I might be on to something.'

'Anything I can do?' There was immediate excitement in the voice. Gerald, who spent his entire life dealing with the peccadilloes of contract-breaking in his show-business legal firm, was fascinated by what he called 'real' crime. He had a Boy's Own Paper enthusiasm for anything shady. 'Wills to check out, blood samples to analyse, stool pigeons to third degree, hit-men to rub out? You name it, I'll do my best.'

Charles wished he could share this detective fiction relish for the case; it all seemed depressingly real to him. 'There is something you can do for me. I'm afraid it involves coming up to Edinburgh.'

'That's all right. One of my clients is in the Actors' Company *Tartuffe*. There's a film contract on the way for him. I could arrange to have to come up and discuss it.'

'Is it urgent?'

'No. But he's not to know that.'

'You mean he's going to be footing your bill?' Charles had to remonstrate on behalf of a fellow actor.

'Don't worry. You should see the money they're paying him for the movie. And he can set me against tax. Really I'm doing him a service.'

'Hmm.' There was never any point in arguing with Gerald on money, it was a subject he had made his own. 'Look, how soon do you think you can get up?'

'If Polly can fix me a flight, I'll be up this evening.' It was typical of Gerald that he would not insult his client's money by contemplating rail travel.

But it was good from Charles's point of view. 'Good. If you can make it, there's a revue I'd like you to see at eleven o'clock. Oh, and could you bring one of your little cassette recorders?'

'Conversation you want to tape?'

'That's it.'

'Secretly?'

'Exactly. Do you think you'll be able to make it tonight?'

'Do my best. Can I ring you back?'

'No, I'm in a call-box.'

'Ring me again in an hour and I'll tell you what gives.'

Charles had decided that he could not face another night with Anna until his suspicions had been exorcised. Then, he kept telling himself, then we can bounce back together again and it'll be even better. Maybe he'd stay in Edinburgh longer than his week. Maybe even away from Edinburgh they could . . .

But not till this was sorted out.

He left the call-box and went down Cockburn Street to the Accommodation Bureau. He picked up his bag from

Coates Gardens and by five o'clock was installed with Mrs Butt in the Aberdour Guest House in Dublin Street, booked for two nights.

He rang Gerald's office from Mrs Butt's pay-phone. Polly's efficiency had worked wonders and her boss was already in a taxi on the way to Heathrow. He would reach the Princes Street terminal in a coach from Edinburgh (Turnhouse) Airport at about ten.

The next move involved seeing Anna. After a couple of bracing whiskies in a Rose Street pub, he went back to Coates Gardens, where, as he anticipated, another cabbage dinner was drawing to its blancmangy end. He signalled to Anna, who left the table discreetly and met him in the empty hall.

The lie slipped out easily. 'Look, I'm sorry. Can't come tonight. An old friend called Alastair Newton came to see the show at lunchtime. He's invited me to dinner at his place. It's some way outside Edinburgh, so he suggested I stay the night there and he'll give me a lift in in the morning. It's a bugger, but I can't really get out of it.'

Anna looked disappointed, which did not make the deception any easier. Then she grinned. 'I could do with some sleep, anyway.'

He grinned too. She was beautiful and the navy blue eyes looked so open and honest, he wished the script of the last few days could be rewritten and all the promptings of suspicion cut out. He felt confident that it would be all right. Probably they would even be able to laugh about it afterwards.

'But tomorrow . . .' he hazarded, 'be O.K. if I come round after the revue as per usual?'

'As per usual. Of course.' There was a lot of warmth in her voice. But she was still discreet and did not want them to be seen together. 'Better get back.'

As she turned to go, he took her hand and leant forward to kiss her. Their lips came together.

A creak on the stairs from the basement made Charles

116

recoil guiltily. Anna as usual kept her cool and glanced towards the person who was staring at them. She looked back at Charles. 'See you then, then.' With unruffled poise she went back to the dining-room. Martin Warburton stood aside to let her pass, looked at Charles, gave one of his abrupt laughs and hurried out of the front door, slamming it behind him.

It didn't matter. Anna was the one who wanted to keep the affair quiet, and somebody was bound to twig sooner or later.

Charles remembered that he had left his toothbrush in the first-floor bathroom. On the landing he met James Milne hurrying angrily downstairs. 'Oh hello, Charles. I've spoken to them before about slamming that door. Not only is it bad for the actual door, it also disturbs the neighbours and I get complaints. Did you see who it was?'

'It was Martin Warburton.'

'Ah.' The Laird's tone changed from angry to confidential. 'Actually I wanted to talk to you about Martin Warburton. Come upstairs and have a drink.'

'Have to be quick. I've got to go out to dinner.' It was important to maintain the lie.

'Won't take long.'

More malt in the leather-bound library. The Laird stood by his marble mantlepiece to give drama to his pronouncement. 'Further to our discussion about Martin's disguise, I followed him this morning.'

'From here?'

'Yes, all the way to Nicholson Street as you described. I waited and he came out with the beard and what have you, and then I followed him again. Guess where he went this time?'

'Not a clue.' Charles found it difficult to get excited about Martin's bizarre doings. He had decided that they were irrelevant to the investigation.

'The Palace of Holyroodhouse,' said James Milne dramatically. 'Now why should he go to the National Portrait Gallery and Holyrood in disguise?'

'I don't know. Maybe he's embarrassed about being a tourist.'

This flippant answer was not well received by the Laird who thought that Martin was definitely the murderer. Charles wished he could share that simple faith; it would be a relief from the forbidding tangle of thoughts that filled his head. But he did not feel inclined to tell his confidant what he knew. It would be better to play along with this Martin theory.

James Milne elaborated. 'I think there's some strange tie-up in his mind. It's all connected with the Mary, Queen of Scots story, I'm sure. Rizzio was only the first of a sequence of murders of people close to that particular lady.'

'I'm a bit hazy about the details of her life. I just remember that she was very tall and when they executed her they lifted the head up and her wig came off.'

'What unusual details you pick on, Charles. I'm sure one of your psychologists would have something to say about the selective processes of your mind. But let me tell you, there's quite a lot more significant stuff in the unfortunate queen's story. I know it fairly well—as a schoolboy I spent one long wet holiday at Glenloan reading everything available on the subject. As you probably know, Mary was the daughter of James V of Scotland and Mary of Guise—'

Charles was in no mood for a schoolmaster's lecture. Worry made him less tolerant than usual. 'James, I'm sorry. I do have to go.'

'Well, let me lend you a book on the subject. I won't give you one of my heavy schoolboy tomes. But there's Antonia Fraser's biography. Popular, but none the worse for that.' His mental catalogue took him straight to the right volume on the shelf.

Charles was eager to leave now. He reached out for the book with muttered thanks, but James Milne kept hold of it and said with a twinkle, 'If I might quote from the Great Unknown, Sir Walter Scott, "Please return this book; I find that though many of my friends are poor arithmeticians, they

are nearly all good bookkeepers." Not a bad joke, considering
the source.'

Charles smiled politely and managed to leave. He was in
no mood for swopping literary references. He found a pub
in Dundas Street where he was unlikely to meet any of the
D.U.D.S. and whiled away the time till Gerald's arrival with
the co-operation of Bell's Whisky, Ltd.

The solicitor arrived at the terminal immaculate in a
Prince of Wales check three-piece suit. He carried an over-
night bag that looked like a giant pigskin wallet and obviously
contained the neatly pressed shirt and pyjamas of a travel
advertisement. 'Hello, buddy. Wise me up on the gen.'

Charles cringed at the number of thrillers Gerald must
have read, and suggested that they talk in a pub.

'Why not in the hotel bar? Then I can check in and dump
the bag.'

'Which hotel?'

'The North British.' It had to be. Typical of Gerald. Polly
had managed to fix it, and somehow the client would manage
to pay for it.

Posh hotels were not Charles's usual style, but whisky's
whisky anywhere. They sat in a dark corner and Gerald
leant towards him conspiratorially. 'O.K. Spill the beans,'
he whispered unsuitably.

'Listen, is your firm engaged in any big film productions
at the moment?'

'We always are. Setting up a colossal Hudson movie out
in Spain. Starts filming in September if we get the contracts
sorted out.'

'Have you got a stake in it?'

'The firm has.' The answer was discreet. Gerald never
admitted his dabbling in film production, though it was
common knowledge that he doubled his already considerable
income by judicious investment.

'So it wouldn't be too difficult for you to pose as a film
producer?'

'It would hardly be a pose,' he replied smugly, and then realised that this was tantamount to an admission of financial interest in films. 'That is, I'm sure I could manage.'

'Right. What I want you to do is to go to a revue called *Brown Derby* at the Masonic Hall in Lauriston Place. It starts at eleven. Now there's a girl in that show called Anna Duncan. She's a good actress, but even if you don't think so, I want you to go round after the performance, introduce yourself as a film producer, say you'd like to talk to her about various ideas and would it be possible to meet for lunch tomorrow.' His treachery tasted foul on his tongue, but it was necessary. He had to know.

Gerald's eyes were sparkling with excitement. 'And tomorrow?'

'You take her out for lunch. I'll fill you in on what to ask her.'

'O.K. And that's the conversation you want recorded?'

Charles nodded. 'If it can be done.'

'No sweat.' The colloquialism again seemed to run counter to the Prince of Wales check. 'Do you think I should use a pseudonym?'

'Don't see why you shouldn't use your own name. If you don't mind.'

'No, of course not.' He was a little crestfallen at losing this dramatic element, but brightened again immediately. 'Is this girl Anna Duncan your Number One Suspect?'

Charles could not bring himself to answer that question, even in his own mind. 'I wouldn't say that. Just need some information from her, that's all. But it's difficult for me to get it myself.'

'Aren't you going to give me all the details of the case so far?'

'Tomorrow. There's no time now. You've got to get to the revue.'

They made a rendezvous for the next morning and Charles went back to the Aberdour Guest House. A half-bottle of

Bell's did not go far enough and he spent a long miserable night with patches of sleep.

Daylight did not speed time up much, and Gerald's arrival at Dublin Street at half-past ten added another delay to the programme. Anna had a tight rehearsal schedule for *Mary* and would not have much of a break for lunch. The assignation had therefore become a dinner date, which extended the agony of waiting by eight hours. Apart from that, all had gone well the previous evening.

Charles then gave Gerald an edited version of the events surrounding Willy Mariello's death and indicated the information he required, with some hints as to what he considered the most effective way of doing it. He hoped that he was judging Anna's character right, and that she would respond in the way he anticipated. But all the time he felt increasingly despicable for the elaborate deception.

At one fifteen he did a performance of *So Much Comic, So Much Blood* without thinking about it. The audience had swelled to nearly eighty and seemed appreciative, but he hardly noticed. He even had a discussion with some dreary Welsh academic about whether Hood's work contained High Moral Seriousness, but only the reflexes of his mind were working. The rest of it was churning with guilt and anxiety.

In the afternoon he tried to pull himself together and entertain thoughts of the other possibilities of the case. What he should really do was to retrace Martin Warburton's visit to Holyrood and see if it prompted any ideas. But even as he thought of it, he knew he could not be bothered. All his thoughts centred on Anna.

As he meandered through the city, he met Frances sitting on a bench in Princes Street Gardens. She had managed to lose Candy and Jane on a sightseeing coach tour of Edinburgh, and was appreciating the break. Charles knew she could tell he was upset, but he refused to unburden himself to her. He knew she would be understanding and reassuring. That was her most infuriating quality, the way she understood him. It was an option he did not want to take. Guilt about Frances joined the mess of unpalatable thoughts in his head.

He hardly listened to what she said. Most of it was about Candy and Jane, the shows they had seen, how exhausting she was finding it, how she'd need a proper holiday after this, how she even thought of staying up in Scotland for a few days to recuperate after the girls had gone. Charles sat, half-hearing and restless. Suddenly he created an appointment and rose. They made vague plans to meet for dinner in the next couple of days when he was clearer about his movements, and he slouched off, not daring to look back at the pain in her eyes.

It was still a long time till the pubs. He approached a cinema, but when he got there changed his mind and continued his aimless perambulation.

At last five o'clock arrived. The whisky did not work. It was as if he had a heavy cold and was numb to its powers. Half past seven came and he thought painfully of Gerald and Anna meeting in the Cosmo Ristorante in North Castle Street. He felt powerless, as if he was watching an accident from too far away to prevent it.

It was nearly ten o'clock when Mrs Butt grudgingly admitted Gerald Venables to the Aberdour Guest House. He was flushed with excitement or wine and carrying a briefcase which contained his cassette recorder. 'Got a specially long tape. I don't know what the quality will be like. I could only put the case on the table and hope for the best.'

Charles was not in the mood for talking. 'Let's hear it.'

Gerald produced the recorder with all the pride of a schoolboy showing his Cycling Proficiency Certificate. He switched the machine on and wound the tape back. Then, as it started, he fiddled with the dials to get the optimum sound.

The quality was not bad. Gerald's own voice was distant because the microphone had been pointing away from him, but he filled in where his original questions were inaudible. There was a lot of interference from dishes being delivered and cutlery clattering, but most of Anna's answers were perfectly clear. Charles got a strange frisson from hearing her voice. It was not attraction exactly, and it was not guilt, but a mixture of emotions he had never encountered before.

The tape started with an amusing dialogue between Gerald and the waiter, who felt certain that Signor would prefer to put his case on the floor. This was followed by the detailed business of ordering. Gerald did not stint himself, and, encouraged by example, nor did Anna. The client in the Actors' Company was certainly going to pay for advice on his film contract.

After these preliminaries, Gerald started explaining why he was in Edinburgh. As a film producer, he was setting up a new movie, meeting some of the other backers, enjoying the Festival . . . and possibly even doing a bit of casting.

Anna's reaction to this was non-committal and Charles began to feel redoubled guilt. If she were innocent what he and Gerald were doing was unforgivable. No aspiring actress should have her hopes manipulated in such a way.

Gerald's distant voice then started to outline the plot of the film he was setting up, according to their plan. He dropped a few suitably substantial names and spoke airily of the locations in Spain and Finland. In fact, it was not all untrue; it was based closely on the film that he really was setting up. The only bit that was complete fabrication was that one part remained uncast. The part of a young girl, whose lover (a considerable film star was playing the part), a terrible lout, treats her cruelly and is stabbed to death halfway through the film. 'Of course,' purred the distant voice, 'that's going to be really difficult, that's the bit that'll call for real acting. The girl's got to express this complex emotion when he's killed. She knows he's a slob, but . . . tricky. I think they should go for Diana Rigg or someone of that stature, but the director's got this crazy idea about finding an unknown. He must've read too many film magazines.'

The first course was delivered. Gerald expertly checked the wine and the sound of Niagara Falls showed that Anna's glass had been adjacent to the microphone. Nothing much happened for a while except for eating and pleasantries. The waiting was purgatory for Charles. Then Gerald's voice resumed its tactics. 'I'm sorry. All this talk of people being stabbed. I read in the papers about that terrible accident in your group. I shouldn't talk about it.'

'It's all right.' Anna's voice came through, very clear and controlled. But was the control genuine, or was there just a fraction too much, a hint of acting?

Gerald continued apologising. 'No, I'm sorry. Shouldn't have mentioned it. It's just that that kind of thing's such a shock. You must have all felt that. But think how much more terrible it must be if the person who dies is a lover or someone close. It doesn't bear thinking of.'

'No. It's terrible.' Charles tried to prise apart the layers of intonation to understand what she meant. Was she rising to the bait? He was torn between the desire to vindicate her and the intellectual satisfaction of having his psychological approach proved right.

Gerald's voice went on, more subdued than ever. 'That's the trouble. Every tragedy leaves someone behind. I suppose this ... Mariello, was that his name? ... I suppose he had a girl somewhere ... oh, it's ghastly ...'

'Yes, he had a girl ...' There was no question about the way she said the line. She played it subtly, wasting none of her talent for drama. But its meaning was undeniably clear. Charles Paris understood that meaning and understanding hurt like physical pain.

Gerald's recorded reactions were unnecessary, but the tape ploughed relentlessly on. 'You mean ... you?'

'Yes. Willy and I were lovers.' The voice was very soft, genuinely moving. There was a long intake of breath and a sob. 'Were ... lovers.'

'I'm so sorry. I had no idea. I wouldn't have raised the matter if I'd had an inkling ...' Gerald's lying protestations

124

continued and Anna's tearful assurances that she had got over it mingled with them. She was playing the scene for all it was worth.

Her unfinished antipasta was taken away and she calmed down sufficiently for the gentle questioning to begin again. 'That must have been absolutely terrible for you. To be there and . . . oh, I'm sorry. And it wasn't that you had been lovers? I mean, you still were right at the end?'

There was a long pause which Charles interpreted as Anna being thrown by the question and not knowing which way to jump. Eventually, the voice came back, quiet, but well projected. 'Yes, right at the end.'

'Good God.' The shock sounded genuine. Gerald had played his part well too. 'You've been thrown into almost exactly the same situation as the girl in this film. It's amazing.' Charles no longer felt guilty about the deceit. Guilt was being forced out of his mind by swelling anger as he listened to Gerald laying the next snare. 'Bereavement is an awful thing. It's so difficult to explain to anyone what you really feel, the true nature of your emotions.

'And of course it's even more complex for the girl in this film. Her lover is, as I said, not very loving. A real bastard, in fact, keeps doing crazy things, cruel things, criminal things. I think the character's overdrawn. No woman would stay with a man like that.'

'I don't know . . .' Again just a simple remark infused with all the art her considerable talent could muster.

'But surely . . .'

'What, all that not speaking ill of the dead business? Why should I worry? He's dead, and when he was alive, it was not his goodness I loved him for. I knew his faults. He could be cruel, oh yes, and evil.' She was warming to her performance. 'He'd do crazy things. Wicked things, and he'd say he'd done them for me.'

Gerald had only to grunt interest; she needed no prompting. 'I mean, take an example. Recently, he nearly killed someone for me. Yes.' She let the drama of it sink in. 'There was a girl in our group who would have been in the revue. She had the part I'm playing. And one day I must have said to Willy that I envied her. I don't mean I was jealous; she was a sweet girl, I liked her—but I must have said what a super part she had or something. And do you know what Willy did?'

'No,' said Gerald, on cue.

'He pushed her down some stone steps.'

'Good God.'

'Yes. It was so cruel. No, I'm sorry, you were wrong when you said I didn't know what it was like to love a bastard. I do, to my cost.'

Charles rose suddenly and switched off the machine.

'She really was very moving,' said Gerald. 'Very. And you reckon this is all significant information? *Cherchez la femme,* that's what they always say in detective stories. Frailty, thy name is woman. Is it Raymond Chandler who calls them frails?'

'Is there much more?' Charles snapped.

'A couple of courses. She did perk up a bit after that.'

'After she'd finished her audition.'

'Yes, I suppose you could say that.'

'I'll spool through and see if there's anything relevant.'

'No, I'll do it, Charles,' said Gerald hastily. 'Incredibly pretty girl, I must say. Sort of navy blue eyes. Do you know her well?'

'I thought I did.'

'Oh.' Understanding dawned. 'Oh.' Gerald busied himself spooling on and playing snatches of the tape. It was mostly general talk about films and the theatre. At one point Charles's ears pricked up.

'. . . had a lot of experience acting?' asked Gerald's voice.

'Yes. Only at university level, of course.'

'But you want to go into the professional theatre?'

'Oh yes. I've had one or two offers.'

'What sort of thing?'

'Well, I've been asked to play Hedda Gabler at the Haymarket, Leicester . . .'

'The cow!' Charles shouted inadequately. With the unquestionable logic of the last piece of a jigsaw puzzle, his own rôle in the proceedings dropped into place. He was just a prop in the oldest theatrical scene of all—the casting couch.

Gerald spooled on and started playing another extract. 'Well, as you know, from last night,' said Anna's voice, 'the show comes down about twelve fifteen and—' He stopped the tape abruptly.

'What was that?' asked Charles.

'Nothing.'

'Switch the damned thing on!' Gerald was powerless against this outburst of fury and sheepishly pressed the button. Anna's voice continued, 'We could meet after that if you like.'

'I'm at the North British down on Princes Street. If you meet me in the foyer, say twelve thirty . . .' Gerald grinned weakly at the sound of his own voice.

'O.K. See you then.' Anna's tone was poisonously familiar.

Charles switched off the recorder and turned to his friend. 'Ah,' said Gerald, 'now don't get the wrong impression. What I thought was, if you were planning a confrontation with her, you'd want to know where she was, and I thought that'd be handy. I mean, for heaven's sake, you didn't think that I'd . . .? I mean, I'm a married man. Kate and I have a perfect relationship and . . .'

He was still mumbling apologetically as Charles stormed out of the room.

At first he just walked furiously without noticing where he was going, but eventually calmed down enough to think of what his next step should be. It was midnight and now a confrontation with Anna was unavoidable. All the delicate feelings which had held him back before had been driven out by anger.

He knew her movements well by now. At twelve fifteen the show came down; he could meet her then at the Masonic Hall. Or he could go back to her flat to wait. But a perverse masochism made him reject both possibilities. At twenty past twelve he took up his position outside the North British Hotel. He leant against the corner of the building, at the top of the steps down to Waverley Station, and prayed she would not come. That at least would spare him the final twist of the knife in his wound. The idea of her deceiving him with Gerald was the most intolerable of all the foul thoughts he was suffering. He would wait till a quarter to one and then go up to the flat.

At twelve thirty she came. He heard the clack of heels and saw the familiar figure walking purposefully along Princes Street towards him. She was wearing the pale yellow shirt with foxtrotting dancers on it and the velvet trousers she had worn when he first took her out to dinner. That made it worse.

As she came close, he shrugged his back off the wall and stepped forward to face her. The pain was too intense for him to find words. He just stood there, rocking on his heels.

Anna did a slight take on seeing him, but when she spoke, her voice was even. 'Charles. Hello. I thought we'd arranged to meet up at the flat.'

He managed to grunt out, 'Yes'.

'It's just as well I've seen you actually, because I won't be there till later. I've got to meet someone in the North British.'

He almost felt respect for the directness of her explanation until the lie followed. 'It's an aunt of mine who's up in Edinburgh very briefly.'

'You're visiting your aunt at twelve thirty a.m. ?'

'Yes. I've been rehearsing all day, so there hasn't been another opportunity. I'll get back to the flat as soon as I can.' She smiled. It was the same smile, the one he had warmed to all week. He realised suddenly that Anna was a perfectly tuned machine. She had all the charm and skills of a human being and knew how to use them like a human being, but inside, controlling everything, was the cold computer of selfishness. Sex, emotions, other people were nothing but programmes to be fed in to produce correct results quickly. Charles knew that he could never again believe anything she said. She was not governed by ordinary principles of truth, but by the morality of advantage.

'You're lying,' he said sharply. 'You're going to the North British to see Gerald Venables. You're going to see him because you think he's a big film producer and can help your career. In the same way that you slept with me because I direct plays, and with Willy Mariello because he was a pop star and might have useful contacts.' He wished the accusations carried some dignity rather than sounding clumsy.

A spark of anger came into the navy blue eyes when she started to speak, but it was quickly smothered. Her voice kept its level tone. 'I see. You set Gerald Venables up?'

'Yes.'

'And he isn't really a film producer? The part he was talking about doesn't exist?'

'He is a sort of occasional film producer. But no, the part doesn't exist.'

She flared. He had hit her where it hurt most, in the career. 'That was a dirty trick.'

For a moment he almost felt a twinge of guilt until he reminded himself of the situation. Anna carried such conviction in her acting. She went on. 'I suppose I should have realised that it was unwise to mix with old men. They only get clinging and jealous.'

That stung him. 'Good God! Do you think I set all this up as some elaborate charade to test your affection for me?' He almost shouted the words. A tweedy middle-aged couple who were passing turned curiously.

'I can't think of any other reason why you should do it.'

That sounded genuine, but then everything she said sounded genuine. Charles was not going to be stopped now. It was a time for truths. And accusations.

'I set Gerald up to get certain information from you.'

'Like what?'

'Like the fact that you and Willy Mariello were lovers.'

'So what? At least he was my age. You see, you are jealous. Jealous of someone who's dead. Anyway, Willy and I were finished. It happened while we were in Derby. We thought it would continue while we were up here, but it didn't.'

'You told Gerald it did, right up to Willy's death.'

'Oh, you've been spying carefully. That wasn't true. I just said that to sound more like the girl in the film.'

That again sounded plausible. The set-up may have been too heavy, and Anna may just have given any information that seemed likely to help her to the part. But Charles was not checked. 'Did Willy want the affair to end?'

'No. He got clinging too. Kept trying to win back my affections. But I'd outgrown him.'

'How did he try to win back your affections?'

'Silly things.'

'Like pushing Lesley Petter down the steps by the Castle?'

That did shake her. There was a long pause before she replied. 'Yes. I suppose that was an attempt to get me back.'

'Did you suggest it?'

'No, I did not!' she snapped. 'I may have mentioned that I was understudying her, that the parts she was playing were good ones, but no . . .'

Charles could imagine her 'mentioning' with all the innocence of Lady Macbeth. 'Listen, Anna, you're in serious trouble.'

'What on earth do you mean?'

'Murder is a serious business.'

'What? Are you accusing me of murder?'

'Yes.'

'You're off your head. Whom am I supposed to have murdered?'

'Willy.'

'Good God.' Now she really did look lost, stunned by the

accusation. 'It never occurred to me that he was murdered. And how in heaven's name am I supposed to have done it? And why, for God's sake?'

'Why first. You incited Willy to nobble Lesley.'

'That's not true. It was his idea.'

'Quite! He did it, thinking that you'd be grateful and bounce back into his arms. It gave him a hold over you and you were forced to go back to him.'

'I didn't.'

'But then he became, as you say, clinging. He was a nuisance, he proved to be without influence in show business circles, but he was not easy to shake off because of your shared guilt over Lesley. So you killed him.'

She was staring at him now in frank amazement. 'And how am I supposed to have done the murder?'

He recapitulated all the business of the knives lying un-attended at Coates Gardens before the killing. 'It was a long chance. The switch was likely to be discovered before the photo-call. But it might work. And it did.'

Anna gave a slight smile. 'But surely, if, as you say, Willy and I were back together, I would have been sleeping at his place and gone straight to the Hall for rehearsal. I wouldn't have gone to Coates Gardens at all during the relevant period.'

That was a blow to Charles' logic. But she had lied so much that she might be lying over that as well. 'You could have crept out in the night.'

'Oh yes, informed by some psychic source that the knives were lying there?'

'Yes,' he asserted, conviction wavering.

'Well, you're wrong. I wasn't sleeping with Willy. But I do have an alibi for the period. I spent that night in the Lawnmarket flat with someone else.'

'Who?'

'Its owner. A bloke called Lestor Wanewright. He was the reason I broke off with Willy. I met him out in Nice while I was on holiday. He has a villa there. We came back here

131

together and he stayed until he had to return to London on business. That was on the morning of Willy's death. Lestor went straight to Waverley Station and I went straight to the Masonic Hall for rehearsal.'

'Why should I believe that?'

'You can check it. Lestor works for his father in London. Wanewright's, the merchant bank.'

'But you took up with me only two days later.'

She shrugged. 'Aren't you flattered?'

'No. You only wanted me for what I could do for you.'

'Yes. I quite liked you too.'

'Oh yes.' There was no danger of his believing anything she said now. Except about Lestor Wanewright. That rang true. If she just wanted an alibi, she had got it with Charles' own assumption that she had been with Willy (a flaw he had overlooked in his argument). The fact that she gave a checkable alibi with Lestor Wanewright meant it was true.

'Goodbye. Charles. I don't think we'll see a lot of each other now.'

'No.'

She walked off, still brisk and purposeful. Lovely, but not human. Charles leant back against the North British Hotel wall and let the warring emotions inside him fight it out for themselves.

One thing he was sure of. Anna Duncan was a dishonest bitch and a whore. But she was not a murderer.

CHAPTER ELEVEN

Even the bright extremes of joy
Bring on conclusions of disgust,
Like the sweet blossoms of the May,
Whose fragrance ends in must.

ODE TO MELANCHOLY

W HEN THE LONG night ended and light returned, Edinburgh had lost its charm. The bubbling spirits with which Charles had arrived had been ebbing for days and the previous evening's events had finally flushed them away. Unsustained by hope and excitement, he felt tired and miserable. And above all, he felt stupid. He saw himself from the outside—a middle-aged man infatuated with a young girl, thinking she could halt the processes of time. He was a figure of fun from a Restoration comedy, the elderly dupe, no doubt dubbed with some unsubtle name like Sir Paltry Effort. The more he thought about the fantasies he'd had of himself and Anna, the way his mind had raced on, the more depressed he felt. Overnight his new lease of life had been replaced by an eviction order.

At about nine he rang Frances. He convinced himself he rang so early to catch her before she went out to the eleven o'clock concert of Mahler songs at Leith Town Hall; not because in his abject state he needed her understanding.

They fixed to meet for dinner, as if it were a casual arrangement. But she knew something had happened and he rang off curtly to stem the flow of sympathy down the phone. He was not ready for that yet.

Then there was Gerald to sort out. Charles did not want to lose a friend over some bloody woman at his age. He went to the North British and summoned the solicitor from a late breakfast.

Gerald came into the hotel foyer wiping his mouth and blushing vigorously. 'Charles, hello,' he said with manufactured bonhomie.

'Hello. I came to thank you for last night.'

'Oh . . . um. It was . . . er . . . nothing. I hope I got you the information you wanted.'

'Yes. It proved I was on the wrong track.'

'Oh, I'm sorry.'

'Mind you, that was a relief in a way.'

'Ah.' Gerald looked at him in silence, uncertainly, as if he half-expected to be punched on the nose. 'Look, old man, about the . . . er . . . other business . . .'

'Forgotten it already.'

'Oh good. But, you know, it's the sort of thing that . . . er . . . well, it was just a joke, but it's the sort of thing . . . I mean, the girl did seem to be virtually offering herself . . .'

'I know.'

'Yes. But it's sort of . . . not the sort of thing to make jokes about. I mean, say you were at home . . . with us. Kate's got a . . . you know . . . a rather limited sense of humour in some ways.'

'It'll never be mentioned.'

'Oh good.' Relief flooded into Gerald and he seemed to swell to fill his expensive suit. 'Care for a cup of coffee?'

When they were seated with their cups, the solicitor started asking about the case.

'I don't know,' Charles replied despondently. 'I was working on the theory that Anna had done it.'

'Good God. I thought you just wanted information out of her.'

'Otherwise you wouldn't have been so anxious to lure her back to your bed?'

'Charles! You said you wouldn't mention it.'

'I'm sorry.'

'So who's the next suspect? Who are you going to turn the heat on now?'

'God knows. I can't think beyond Anna. All my other lines of enquiry are confused. Anyway, my last performance is tomorrow. Now all I want to do is get the hell out of Edinburgh.'

'But what about the case?'

'I don't even know if there is a case. Suppose Willy Mariello died by an accident? That's what everyone else thinks. Why shouldn't they be right?'

'But Charles, your instinct—'

'Bugger my instinct. Look, even if it wasn't an accident, who cares? No one's mourned Willy much. One slob less, what does it matter if he was murdered? It's certainly not my business.'

'You mustn't take that attitude.'

'Why not?' he snapped. 'I'm an actor, not a detective. If I were a detective, I'd have been sacked years ago for incompetence. There are some things one can do and some one can't. It's just a question of recognising that fact before you make a fool of yourself. And I now know that I have as much aptitude for detective work as a eunuch has for rape.'

'So you don't think you'll pursue the case?'

'No.'

'Hmm. I'm getting a plane back shortly.'

'Yes. Well, thanks for your help.'

'It was nothing.'

'See you in London, Gerald.'

'And if you change your mind, and do go on investigating, let me know how you get on.'

'Sure. Cheerio.' Charles slouched out of the hotel.

Apparently he did a reasonable performance of *So Much Comic, So Much Blood* to an audience of one hundred and twenty at lunchtime. He did not really notice it. All he was thinking was how soon he could get out of Edinburgh.

That involved tying up professional loose ends. Which

meant a call on Brian Cassells at Coates Gardens. Charles hoped that the *Mary* cast were rehearsing at the Masonic Hall; he did not want to meet Anna Duncan. Ever again.

His hope proved justified. The house was unusually quiet. The Company Manager was in his office, as usual pressing Letraset on to sheets of paper. 'Thought we might need a bit of puff for *Who Now?* Opens on Monday in your lunchtime slot. Got to keep ahead in the publicity game or no one knows a show's on.'

'No, they don't,' said Charles pointedly, thinking of the publicity his show had got.

But irony was wasted on Brian. 'I've changed "A Disturbing New Play" to "A Macabre and Bloody Exposition of Violence by Martin Warburton". Pity I have to hint; I'd like to add ". . . who stabbed Willy Mariello". That'd really bring the audience in. Still, the police are probably still investigating, so we may get some more publicity.'

Charles searched the Company Manager's face for a trace of humour after this pronouncement, but it was not there. ' "Stabbed to death" rather implies a positive act, like murder, Brian. Doesn't fit in with an accident.'

It was a half-hearted attempt to see if the average member of D.U.D.S. harboured any suspicions about Willy's death. Brian obviously did not. 'Oh, that's just semantics. You mustn't get too hung up on meaning, you've got to think of the impact of words.'

'Hmm. Are you going into advertising?'

'I might think of it if I don't get this Civil Service job I'm up for.'

'You'd be very good at it.'

'Thank you.' Again totally unaware that a remark could be taken two ways.

'Actually I wanted to talk about money.' They arranged that Brian would send a cheque to London when the miserable fifty per cent of the miserable box office was worked out. Charles was not expecting much; in fact he could work out exactly how much by simple arithmetic; but he preferred not to. That always left the possibility of a pleasant surprise.

But he knew the payment would not begin to cover his expenses. It hurt to think how much lavish meals for Anna figured on those expenses. The classic fall-guy, the duped sugar-daddy—he felt a wave of self-distaste.

Have to make some more money somehow. Maybe the B.B.C. P.A.s' strike would soon be over and the telly series would happen. It was the first time he had thought outside Edinburgh since he arrived. A line echoed in his mind. 'There is a world elsewhere.' Was it Shakespeare? He could not recall. But it was melancholy and calming.

He hoped to leave Coates Gardens without meeting James Milne, but failed. So he was left with the unattractive prospect of Sherlock Holmes telling Dr Watson that he had given up investigation.

'Anything new?' the Laird hissed eagerly as they met in the hall. He swivelled his white head left and right in an elaborate precaution against eavesdroppers. Charles was getting sick of enthusiastic amateur sleuths—Gerald with his inept slang, James Milne with his melodramatic whispering.

'No, not a lot.' He tried unsuccessfully to make it sound as if that exhausted the subject.

'You haven't been following Martin again?'

'No, I've . . . er . . . no.' He had not mentioned any suspicions of Anna to his confidant and it seemed pointless to start just as the Dr Watson rôle was becoming redundant.

'But you must have been following some line of investigation the last couple of days.'

'Yes, I have, but I . . . don't really want to talk about it.'

'Something personal?'

'Yes, I found it involved someone I knew well and . . .' He hoped that might edge the conversation in another direction. The Laird's old-fashioned values would surely respect a chap's discretion about his private affairs. I mean, dash it all, when there's a lady in the case . . .

But James Milne's curiosity was stronger than his

gentlemanly outlook. 'And where are those suspicions leading you?' he asked with some excitement.

'Nowhere. Well, I mean they've led anywhere they're going to lead. And produced nothing. I just want to forget about the case now.'

The Laird looked at him quizzically. 'But you were so keen on it before. I mean, it was your idea that there was anything to investigate. And now you've managed to persuade me there's something in it. You can't just drop it.'

'I can. I have.'

'But don't you think we ought to do some more investigation of Martin's movements and behaviour?'

'Sorry. I've lost interest.'

'Oh. And you're leaving tomorrow?'

'Yes.'

'Ah. Well, I'd better return your Hood.' James Milne ignored Charles's remonstrance that it didn't matter, found the volume immediately and handed it over.

'Enjoy it?' Charles saw a way out of the awkwardness into the impersonal area of literary criticism.

'Yes,' came the morose reply.

'Amazing feeling for words.'

'Yes.'

'There's a lot of discussion as to whether it's a purely comic gift. I mean, in some cases a pun does reinforce a serious statement. You know, like that line from *A Friendly Address to Mrs Fry*. "But I don't like your *Newgatory* teaching." '

'Yes.' The Laird responded in a predictably brighter tone.

Charles pressed home his advantage. 'And some of the wholly serious poems aren't bad. Did you try *The Plea of the Midsummer Fairies*?'

'Yes. Sub-Keats, I thought.'

'Right. But *The Song of the Shirt's* O.K. if hackneyed, and *The Bridge of Sighs* is quite moving. And did you read *The Dream of Eugene Aram*?'

'No,' said the Laird, 'I've never heard of it,' and relapsed into gloom. Charles felt churlish for his proposed defection.

He needed to soften the blow of his departure. 'Look, let's meet for a farewell drink in the morning. At the pub by the Masonic Hall. See you there about eleven. Before my last lunchtime. O.K.?'

The Laird nodded, but he looked downcast and Charles felt that he had let the man down.

Dinner with Frances was refreshing in that, unlike Gerald Venables and James Milne, she did not encourage him to continue with his detective work. In fact, when he gave her a selective résumé of his investigations, she positively discouraged him. Murder, in her view, was an extremely unpleasant business, and when inadvertently it did occur, it belonged by right to the police and not to untrained amateurs. It could be very dangerous. Although they were separated, Frances retained a maternal protective instinct for her husband. This regularly manifested itself in warm socks and sensible Marks and Spencer shirts for birthdays and Christmas.

They ate in Henderson's Salad Bar, a bit of a comedown from the places where he had squired Anna, but excellent food and better value. Charles began to relax. As he did, the exhaustion that had been stalking him all day caught up. He nearly nodded asleep into his lentil stew. Frances reached out and held his hand. 'You're dead.'

'Mmm.'

'Been overdoing it.'

'I suppose so.'

'Early night.'

'Good idea.'

'I'm pretty exhausted too. Those two girls have been leading me such a dance. Still, thank God they get a train back tomorrow. It can't come soon enough. I think I might stay in Scotland for a bit.'

'Don't you have to chaperone them home?'

'No. Put the two little horrors on the London train and from that moment they're on their own.'

Charles smiled weakly at the incipient relief in her voice. 'And then you'll have a few days' holiday?'

'Yes. Bliss. Before term starts.' She hesitated. 'I don't suppose . . .'

'What?'

'I don't suppose you'd fancy a few days' holiday. If we could book up somewhere . . .'

It was strange to see her blushing. Blushing for propositioning her own husband. He felt the familiar ridge of the kitchen-knife scar across her thumb. His eyelids were heavy with sleep as he replied. 'I've heard worse ideas.'

There was quite a party at the pub before Charles's performance on the Saturday. A lot of the D.U.D.S. who had never said hello to him decided they had an obligation to say goodbye, and any money that the show might have made was anticipated in large rounds of drinks for people he did not know.

But Charles didn't mind. A night's sleep had done wonders. Alcohol and company meant that he only felt the occasional twinge from thoughts of Anna or Willy's death. Recovery from both obsessions would take time, but it was possible.

Frances was there, celebrating the departure of a King's Cross train from Waverley Station. And, by a stroke of incredible luck, they had arranged a holiday. Stella Galpin-Lord, who was in the party, justified the expense of the vodka and Campari she ordered by fixing them up in a hotel at Clachenmore on Loch Fyne. In fact she had been booked in for a week herself, but had just heard that the acting friend who was meant to join her had got a part in a film and had to cancel. The need for a consoling drink after this disappointment explained her presence in the pub. But her loss was Charles's and Frances's gain. A phone call clinched the change of booking. Charles was so excited about the speed with which it happened that he did not have time to question the wisdom of going on holiday with his ex-wife.

He felt affectionate towards all of the Derby crowd and, now that his departure was imminent, even indulged himself in a slight regret that it was over. Sam Wasserman was talking earnestly (and no doubt allegorically) to Pam Northcliffe. She had her back to Charles, but he could imagine the glaze of boredom slowly covering her eyes. Frances was gamely trying to conduct a conversation with the lighting man Plug (who'd got to do the sodding cue sheets for *Who Now?*, but who'd heard there was a free drink going). Martin Warburton was gesticulating wildly as he expounded one of his theories to Stella Galpin-Lord. They all seemed animated and cheerful except for James Milne who sat slightly apart with a half of 'heavy'.

Since the Laird was the first person he'd invited to the get-together, Charles felt he should not neglect him and sat down at the same table with his pint.

'Are you really giving the investigation up, Charles?'

He found it difficult to meet the older man's eyes. 'Yes.'

'I'm sure we ought not to. I mean, if something else happens, we'll feel terrible.'

'What else can happen?'

'Another crime.'

'Why?'

'I don't know. It's just . . .' The Laird leant closer and whispered. 'I am convinced there's something odd about Martin's behaviour. We ought to find out more. We can't just leave it.'

This was unsettling. Deep down Charles agreed. But he had managed to push that agreement so far down that it hardly troubled him. He would have to make some concession to his conscience. 'What, you mean investigate the flat in Nicholson Street?'

'Something like that, Charles.'

'How about Holyrood?' With sudden inspiration. 'We'll go this afternoon.' The Laird looked relieved that something was being done and Charles felt it was a satisfactory solution.

It gave the illusion of interest on his part and was a pleasant way of spending an afternoon. A visit to Edinburgh's famous palace would be a fitting farewell to the city.

'Drink?' The word was spoken sharply close behind Charles. He turned to see Martin Warburton holding a couple of empty glasses. 'I'm getting a round.'

Charles looked at his watch. 'Better not have any more. I'll want a pee in the middle of the show.'

James Milne also refused politely, but Martin did not turn away immediately. He stood still for a moment and said, almost to himself, 'Holyrood.'

'Yes,' said Charles. 'We're going down there this afternoon.' And then, as an explanatory probe, 'Have you ever been there?'

'Oh no,' Martin replied slowly. 'No, I haven't.'

The last performance of *So Much Comic, So Much Blood* went very well; it justified the *Glasgow Herald*'s enthusiasm. It was possibly helped by the alcoholic relaxation of its presenter, and certainly by the vigorous reactions of an alcoholic contingent in the audience. Charles was left with the melancholy emptiness that follows a good show, and an urgent awareness that the pubs closed at two thirty.

A few more drinks and he parted with the D.U.D.S. in a haze of goodwill. Frances went off to scour Edinburgh for gumboots which she assured Charles would be essential for the West Coast of Scotland. James Milne waited for him outside the Masonic Hall while he slipped in to have another pee and pick up his belongings.

The stage crew were already in, setting up the scenery for a lighting rehearsal of *Who Now?* Martin Warburton, as writer, was deep in conference with Plug, the electrician. Charles picked up the holdall that he had left onstage. 'Did all the slides go in, Plug?'

'Sure.'

'Cheerio then.'

' 'Bye.' Charles swung the holdall cheerfully on to his shoulder.

'Goodbye, Charles Paris,' said Martin Warburton.

The guide at the Palace of Holyroodhouse was a jovial gentleman with a green cap, green jacket and tartan trews. The effort of showing a mixed bag of international tourists round the old building ten times a day (or even more during the Festival) had not blunted his good humour, though it did give a staged quality to some of his jokes.

Charles let it all wash pleasantly over him. He even felt confident that the alcohol would not wear off until the pubs opened again at five. After the stresses of recent days he owed himself a real Saturday night blinder.

Meanwhile information about Scotland's history and art poured out from the guide. Charles II rebuilt the palace . . . George IV wanted to be painted wearing a kilt . . . you can tell the carving's by Grinling Gibbons because of his signature of five peas in a pod . . . the present Queen holds garden parties in the gardens here . . . the harpsichord by Johann Rucker of Antwerp is still in working order . . . the portraits of fictitious kings of Scotland are by Jacob de Wet . . . and so on and so on.

Occasionally Charles would be shaken from his reverie by a hiss from the Laird. 'Do you think that might be significant?'

'What?'

'Sixteenth-century tapestry of the Battle of the Centaurs.'

'Why?'

'Well, it's violent, isn't it? And Martin's very obsessed with violence.'

Charles would feign interest for a moment and then mentally doze off again. With the confidence of alcohol, he knew that so far as he was concerned the Mariello case was over. The relief of that decision gave him the freedom to look at the case objectively. He saw the long trail of his mistaken suspicions dragging on like a Whitehall farce, with him as the overacting protagonist, always opening the wrong door after the crooks had fled, after the pretty girl had put her clothes back on again, or after the vicar's trousers had been irrevocably lost.

And, without the pressure of having to think about it, a new logic crept into the case. First, the greatest likelihood was that Willy Mariello had died accidentally. And if he had not, then the only person with whom he was directly connected was James Milne, through the house sale. Perhaps there had been some motive there; perhaps even (taking a cue from Michael Vanderzee's insinuation) there had been a homosexual liaison between Willy and the Laird. Perhaps, perhaps. Motivations and suspicions took on the expendable and detached fascination of a crossword. Perhaps one day someone would make the effort to find out the facts. Preferably a policeman. Certainly it would not be Charles Paris. Detective work, he reflected, was a slow and unrewarding business, like reading Dickens for the dirty bits. Not for him. He followed the guide through a film of alcohol.

The oldest parts of Holyroodhouse, in the James IV Tower, are kept till last in the guided tour. These are the apartments of Mary, Queen of Scots and her second husband, Lord Darnley, and it is impossible to enter them without a sense of excitement.

Darnley's bedroom is downstairs and there is a little staircase that leads up to the Queen's room. Next door is the supper room where David Rizzio, her Italian secretary, musician and companion, was murdered by Darnley, Patrick Lord Ruthven and other disaffected noblemen. On his body there were found between fifty and sixty dagger-wounds.

'And there,' said the guide dramatically, 'is the very spot where it happened.' Then, with a quick switch into the practised joke, 'There's no use looking for bloodstains. There's only a brass plaque there and it's a different floor. But everything else is just as it was.'

'Everything?' Charles queried facetiously. 'Is it the same clock?'

'What clock?' asked the guide, confused for the first time on the tour.

'Well, the clock . . .' Charles turned slowly round the room. There was no clock. 'Then what's the ticking?'

He looked slowly down at his holdall, lowered it to the floor and, with great care, unzipped it. The other tourists watched with frozen fascination.

There was no question. He had seen enough newspaper pictures from Northern Ireland to recognise the untidy arrangement of a clock face and wires.

So had the rest of the party. In the panic and screams that followed as they all rushed for the narrow spiral staircase, he could hear the Laird's voice, high with fear. 'A bomb! He could have killed us all! A bomb!'

CHAPTER TWELVE

The dog leapt up, but gave no yell,
The wire was pulled, but woke no bell,
The ghastly knocker rose and fell,
  But caused no riot;
The ways of death, we all know well,
  Are very quiet.

JACK HALL

Bombs in public places are police matters, and cannot be well investigated by half-hearted amateurs. Charles found it a great relief when the blue uniforms moved in. He felt he could have gone on snooping in the dark for ever; the police had the advantage that investigation was their business. And they got on with it very efficiently.

An Army bomb disposal expert saved Queen Mary's historic apartments from destruction. As Charles sat waiting to be interviewed at the Edinburgh City Police Headquarters in Fettes Avenue, he wondered what would have happened if the device had gone off. The wholesale destruction of twenty-odd tourists and a guide might have put Rizzio's murder in the shade. And it would have needed a hell of a big brass plaque.

He had assumed that the bomb had not reached its detonation time when it was discovered and received an ugly shock when the findings of the bomb disposal expert were communicated to him. It had been set for twenty minutes earlier. The minute hand on the clock had reached its brass contact screw fixed in the clock face; it was only luck that had prevented it going off. The device's construction was amateur and the motion of Charles' holdall appeared to have broken one of the inadequately soldered joints in the wiring. But for the cavalier, drunken way he had manhandled the bag, the bomb would have worked.

He found its failure small comfort. The intention was no less destructive. The bomb was an unsophisticated weed-killer and acid device, which might not have been too devastating in the open, but in an enclosed space like the supper room . . . He didn't like to think about it. Particularly as he had been carrying the thing. Even in the unlikely event of his surviving the blast, he would have been typecast for the rest of his life as Long John Silver or Toulouse-Lautrec.

When he talked to the police, he was amazed at how much they knew. The assumption that they had written off Willy Mariello's death as an accident and were just waiting for this to be officially confirmed in the Procurator-Fiscal's report proved to be naïve. Ever since the stabbing they had been investigating and keeping an eye on the D.U.D.S. They knew about Martin's dual identity and had been following his movements with particular interest.

It all made Charles feel crassly amateur. Not only because his own stumbling investigations seemed so pathetic, but also because it showed he had an outdated image of the police as thick village constables whose only function was to have rings run round them by the brilliant amateur sleuth. That was the way it was in most of the plays he had ever been in, and plays were about his closest contact with the police. What he had taken in this case to be their lethargic inactivity had been discreet investigation, gathering together sufficient evidence for an arrest.

And they reckoned the bomb was probably enough evidence. Certainly enough to justify a search of the flat in Nicholson Road.

There was no question in the police's mind of investigating anyone but Martin. Like the Laird, they reckoned that his behaviour was suspicious and, unlike Charles, they were not held up by vague woolly liberal notions that the boy was misunderstood and must have other explanations for his actions. Charles felt as he had in Oxford when, after an elaborate midnight climb back into college over walls, across roofs, down drainpipes and through dons' bedrooms, he had discovered that the main gate was open.

He also felt rather out of it, though at the centre of operations. At least on his own abortive investigations he could maintain the illusion of doing something important in his own right. Here at the police headquarters he was just a source of information, politely asked to wait, filed for reference when necessary. They were interested in what he knew, not what he thought.

So rather than stage-managing dramatic dénouements himself, he found out at second hand what had happened. The search at Nicholson Street had provided plenty of evidence to convict Martin. It was a positive bomb factory, chemicals and components scattered around on tables without any attempt at concealment. There was also an unpleasant collection of knives and other weapons, including a meat cleaver. The boy's fantasies of violence took a disturbingly tangible form.

What the police did not find at the flat was Martin Warburton himself. And, though they found a bottle of spirit gum substitute and a brush, there was no sign of his false beard or glasses. So it was possible that he was somewhere in Edinburgh in his disguise.

They tried the obvious places, which were Coates Gardens and the Masonic Hall, but he was not at either. Apparently he had left the theatre after a disagreement with Plug over some lighting effect. That was shortly before three, and nobody had seen him since.

The case had changed from a whodunnit to a manhunt.

Charles was thanked courteously for his co-operation by the police and asked to keep them informed of where he would be contactable if he left Edinburgh.

It was then about seven o'clock. Frances, he knew, had got a ticket for the Scottish Opera's *Alceste* at the King's Theatre. Denied her calming therapy for his shattered nerves, he saw no reason to change his plans of earlier in the day, and got drunk.

At the Police Headquarters James Milne and Charles had arranged to meet for coffee in the flat the next morning to talk through what had happened. Charles had found the truth of Dr Johnson's dictum about the proximity of death concentrating a man's mind wonderfully, and regained his flagging interest in the case.

About eleven on the Sunday he arrived at Coates Gardens. 'Do you mind if I have something a bit stronger than coffee?'

'Still in a state of shock? So am I.'

'Well, mine's only an indirect state of shock, James. I was so shocked yesterday that I had to have a great deal to drink for medical reasons. That's why I need something stronger now. Hair of the dog.'

The Laird chuckled and reached for the malt whisky bottle. 'Well,' he said when they were sitting and the first gulp was irrigating Charles's dehydrated head, 'it seems that I was on the right track.'

'About Martin?'

'Yes.'

'Hmm. Of course, I knew there was something wrong with him right from the start. Now I come to think of it, the first night I was here, I heard someone crying in the bathroom— I'm sure it was him. Obviously in the throes of a nervous breakdown. A schizoid condition, aggravated by overwork for his finals.'

'All work and no play . . .'

'Makes Jack a nutter, yes.'

' "Much study had made him very lean . . ." '

' "And pale and leaden-eyed." ' Charles completed the quotation automatically without thinking. Martin's case seemed more relevant than literary games. 'What surprised me was that all his fantasies manifested themselves in a real way. Usually with that type all the action's in their minds.'

'Not, it seems, in this case, Charles.'

'No.' He paused for a moment, ruefully. 'Poor kid. He was so mixed up. He seemed so much the obvious suspect that I never really considered him.' He laughed. 'I must get a less subjective view of criminals.'

'What do you mean?'

'Look at me—on this case I miss out the obvious solution just because Martin's someone I like and feel sympathy for. Instead I go off into wild suspicions of more or less everyone else I meet.' The atmosphere between them was friendly enough for a confession. 'Do you know, I even suspected you at one point.'

'Really? Why?'

'God knows. My mind wasn't working very well. I suspected everybody. Still, even if we didn't know about Martin's bomb factory, I think I'd have to cross you off my list now. The average murderer doesn't deliberately try to get himself blown up.'

'No.' They laughed.

Then Charles sighed. 'I wish I'd got it all a bit more sorted out in my mind. I mean, it's now clear that Martin planted the bomb, and presumably planned Willy's death as well, but I still don't see exactly why.'

'He was unbalanced.'

'Yes, but . . . I don't know. I suppose I've got a tidy mind, but I'd like to find some sort of method in his madness, some logical sequence.'

'What about the Mary, Queen of Scots thing I suggested a few days ago?'

'That would explain the Mariello stabbing, I suppose. Willy was playing Rizzio, so there might be some identification there, but what about the bomb?'

'Darnley was blown up with gunpowder, Charles.'

'Was he? Good God.'

'Yes, I'm sure he was. At the instigation of Bothwell, as I recall.'

'Bothwell? But that's who Martin's playing in *Mary,*

Queen of Sots. And . . . yes . . . he talked to me once about how easy it was to identify with people from history.'

'There you are then.'

'Let's work it out. He's in this show about Mary, Queen of Scots and gets obsessively involved with her life . . .'

'A life surrounded by intrigue and murder.'

'Exactly. He identifies with Bothwell and—I say, it's just struck me. I bet there's a portrait of Bothwell in the Scottish National Portrait Gallery.'

The Laird nodded excitedly. 'There is. It's a miniature. And it's the only extant picture of him.'

'Yes.' Charles pieced it together slowly. 'Right. Martin identifies so completely that, in his confused mind, he becomes Bothwell and Sam Wasserman's awful play becomes reality. And that reality suits his existing obsessions about violence.'

'So Rizzio has to be stabbed. Willy Mariello doesn't exist for Martin; he actually is David Rizzio. And Martin must have said something that made Willy afraid of him, which explains what Willy told me in the Truth Game. By a stroke of luck, the stabbing looks like an accident, and so Martin is free to plan his next murder, that of Darnley . . .' His racing thoughts were suddenly brought up short. 'But that's strange. If he was living the reality of the play, why did he identify me with Darnley and not the bloke who's actually playing the part?'

'Perhaps he was just getting a bit confused,' the Laird offered.

'That's a bit lame. I'm sure if the obsession's as complicated as it seems to be, there must be some logic behind it, some sort of crazy justification for his action.'

'You don't think there's anything missing in the historical Mary story?'

'I don't know. What happened to Bothwell in the end?'

'I think he died in prison. Insane.'

Charles smiled grimly. 'I'm afraid that part of the

identification could be horribly apt too. No, there's something we're missing. Why does he turn on me as Darnley?'

'Because he thinks you're on his trail?'

'Doesn't really fit the historical obsession bit. Unless . . .' The solution flashed into his mind. 'Good God! Anna!'

'What?'

'Anna Duncan. She's playing Mary. And Willy Mariello had an affair with her. Martin must have seen them together and killed him out of jealousy. And then me. He saw us together downstairs a couple of days ago.'

'You and Anna?'

Charles felt himself blushing, but the picture was developing too quickly for him to be discreet. 'Yes, we were having an affair, and after he saw us together, he started to identify me with Darnley. So I had to be blown up.'

'Leaving Anna to him?'

'I suppose so. But don't you see, James, this may give us a lead on what he's likely to do next.'

'Why?'

'Who's the next person to be murdered in the Mary, Queen of Scots saga?'

The Laird pondered with infuriating slowness. 'Well, I think actual murders are a bit thin on the ground after Darnley. There are plots and battles, but I don't think any more major figures were actually murdered.'

'None at all?'

'No. Well, not until Mary herself had her head cut off. There are a lot of Scots who still regard that as a murder.'

Charles sprang to his feet with a feeling of nausea in his throat. 'No! I must get to the Lawnmarket.' All he could think of was the fact that among other weapons in the Nicholson Street flat the police had found a meat cleaver.

He was so relieved to see Anna open the door of the flat that it took a moment before he realised the situation's inherent awkwardness. She looked at him and the Laird without emotion. 'Good morning.'

Urgency overcame Charles' embarrassment. 'Have you seen Martin?'

'Yes.'

'What, here?'

'Yes, he was here.'

'When?'

'He left about half an hour ago.'

'And how long had he been here?'

A hard look came into the navy blue eyes. 'Listen, if you're playing another of your elaborate games—'

'I'm not. This is serious. We've got to find Martin. He's in a dangerous state.'

'Certainly in a strange state. He was babbling on about the police being after him or something.'

'That's true.'

'Why?'

'They want him for the murder of Willy Mariello and the attempted murder of Charles Paris.'

Her mouth fell open and an expression of frozen horror came over her face. Charles realised it was the first spontaneous reaction he had ever seen from her.

'Where is he now?'

'I don't know, Charles. He came here last night in an awful state and begged to stay. I thought he was mad, so I didn't argue.'

'Just as well. I think you were next on his list.'

'What?' She started to cry with shock, and looked human and ugly. But Charles did not have time to notice. 'Have you any idea where he was going?'

'No, but he was dressed up.'

'Disguised?'

'Yes. I thought he was joking when he suggested it, but he was so fierce and insistent that I let him have the stuff.'

'What stuff?'

'A smock and a handbag of mine. And a curly dark wig I've got. And my sunglasses.'

'He was wearing all that when he left?'

'Yes.'

'Thank you.' He turned to rush away.

'Charles?' she whispered.

'Yes.'

'Do you think he really might have murdered me?'

'Yes, Anna. I do.'

As he ran down the steps from Lady Stair's Close towards Waverley Station, he knew it was a long chance, but he could not think of anywhere else to go. If Martin wanted to get out of Edinburgh, that was the quickest way. Charles had a feeling that there was a London train at two o'clock. In twenty minutes.

The cold sweaty feeling of his hangover mixed with the hot sweaty feeling of running. Ambling tourists turned bewildered faces towards the middle-aged man pelting down the road in the calm of a Sunday afternoon. James Milne was a long way behind him, doing the ungainly penguin run of a man with things in his pockets.

Charles sped down the taxi-ramp into Waverley Station and halted in the sudden cool shade, gasping to get his breath. Then he moved slowly towards Platform 1/19 where the London train would leave. It had not yet arrived.

He stalked along the railings that ran the length of the platform and peered through at the passengers, who stood waiting with their luggage. They all looked extremely ordinary. He walked on. The women were very womanly.

He stopped and looked at one back view again. The clothes were right. Red smock, blue jeans, curly hair, handbag dangling casually from one hand. It must be.

But he hesitated. There was something so feminine about the stance. And no trace of anxiety.

But it must be. Martin's chameleon-like ability to take on another personality would enable him to stand differently, to think himself so much into the part that he was a woman. Any actor could do it to a degree and a psychopath could do it completely.

154

Charles moved with organised stealth. He bought a platform ticket and walked through the barrier. Then he advanced slowly towards the 'woman'. People peered along the line and started to gather up their luggage. The train was coming. He quickened his pace.

He was standing just behind his quarry when the train slid protesting into the station. Even close to, the figure looked womanly. Charles waited a moment; he did not want to risk a suicide under the oncoming wheels. But as the passing windows slowed to a halt, he stepped forward. The curly head was close to his face. 'Martin,' he said firmly.

The violence of the blow on his chest took him by surprise. He had time to register the skill of the boy's make-up as he fell over backwards.

The shove winded him and it was a moment before he could pick himself up again. By that time Martin had charged the barrier and was rushing through the dazed crowd in the main station. Charles set off in gasping pursuit.

The boy was at least two hundred yards ahead when Charles emerged into the sunlight, and running up the hill which the older man had just descended. Martin was young and fit and moving with the pace of desperation. Charles was hopelessly out of condition on the steep gradient and could feel the gap between them widening.

Then he had what seemed like a stroke of luck. Martin was keeping to the right of the road as if he intended to veer off down the Mound into Princes Street where he would soon be lost in the tourist crowds. But suddenly he stopped. Charles could see the reason. James Milne was standing in his path. Martin seemed frozen for a moment, then sprang sideways, crossed the road and ran on up the steps to the Lawnmarket, retracing Charles' footsteps.

In fact, going straight back to Anna's flat.

Realisation of the girl's danger gave Charles a burst of adrenalin, and he surged forward. As he passed the Laird on the steps he heard the older man gasp something about getting the police.

Martin was spreadeagled against the door in Lawnmarket ·
when Charles emerged from Lady Stair's Close. The boy was
hammering with his fists, but Anna had not opened the door
yet. No doubt she was on her way down the five flights of
steps. Charles screamed out Martin's name, turning the
heads of a party of Japanese in tam o'shanters.

The youth turned round as if he had been shot and froze
again like a rabbit in a car's headlights, unable to make up
his mind. Charles moved purposefully forward. It had to be
now; he had no energy left for a further chase.

He was almost close enough to touch Martin, he could
see the confusion in the young eyes, when suddenly the youth
did another sidestep and started running again. Charles
lumbered off in pursuit, cursing. If Martin made it down to
the Grassmarket, he could easily lose his exhausted hunter
in the network of little streets of the Old Town.

But Martin did not do that. He did something much more
worrying.

Instead of breaking for the freedom of the Grassmarket,
he ran back across the road and up towards the Castle.
In other words, he ran straight into a dead end. With a new
cold feeling of fear, Charles hurried after him, up between
the Tattoo stands on the Esplanade and into the Castle.

The fear proved justified. He found Martin standing on
the ramparts at the first level, where great black guns point
out over the New Town to the silver flash of the Firth of
Forth. A gaping crowd of tourists watched the boy in silence
as he pulled off the wig and smock and dropped them into
the void.

Charles eased himself up on to the rampart and edged
along it, trying not to see the tiny trees and beetle people in
Princes Street Gardens below. 'Martin.'

The look that was turned on him was strangely serene.
So was the voice that echoed him. 'Martin. Yes, Martin.
Martin Warburton. That's who I am.' The youth wiped
the lipstick from his mouth roughly with the back of his

hand. 'Martin Warburton I began and Martin Warburton I will end.'

'Yes, but not yet. You've got a long time yet. A lot to enjoy. You need help, and there are people who will give you help.'

Martin's eyes narrowed. 'The police are after me.'

'I know, but they only want to help you too.' This was greeted by a snort of laughter. 'They do. Really. We all want to help. Just talk. You can talk to me.'

Martin looked at him suspiciously. Charles felt conscious of the sun, the beautiful view of Edinburgh spread out below them. A peaceful Sunday afternoon in the middle of the Festival. And a young man with thoughts of suicide. 'Don't do it, Martin. All the pressures you feel, they're not your fault. You can't help it.'

'Original Sin,' said the boy, as if it were a great joke. 'I am totally evil.'

'No.'

For a moment there was hesitation in the eyes. Charles pressed his advantage. 'Come down from there and talk. It'll all seem better if you talk about it.'

'Talk? What about the police?' Martin was wavering.

'Don't worry about the police.'

Martin took a step towards him. Their eyes were interlocked. The boy's were calm and dull; then suddenly they disengaged and looked at something over Charles' shoulder. Charles turned to see that two policemen had joined the edge of the growing crowd.

When he looked back, he saw Martin Warburton launch himself forward like a swimmer at the start of a race.

But there was no water and it was a long way down.

And Brian Cassells got another good publicity story.

CHAPTER THIRTEEN

A plague, say I, on all rods and lines, and on young
    or old watery danglers!
And after all that you'll talk of such stuff as no harm
    in the world about anglers!
And when all is done, all our worry and fuss, why,
    we've never had nothing worth dishing;
So you see, Mr Walton, no good comes at last of your
    famous book about fishing.

           A RISE AT THE FATHER OF ANGLING

CHARLES WATCHED THE sun-gold surface of the burn
change in seconds to dull brown and then become pock-
marked with heavy drops of rain. He heard a rustle of
P.V.C. behind him as Frances tried to rearrange her position at the foot of the tree to keep the maximum amount of
water off her book. The rain was no less cheering than the
sun.

As he knew from previous experience, if you do not like
rain, there's no point in going to the West Coast of Scotland.
The whole area is wet. Wet underfoot like the surface of a
great sponge. Everywhere the ground is intersected with tiny
streams and it is never completely silent; there is always the
subtle accompaniment of running water. The wetness is not
the depressing damp of soggy socks and smelly raincoats; it
is stimulating like the sharp kiss of mist on the cheek. And
it is very relaxing.

Charles twitched his anorak hood over his head and
thought how unrelaxed he still felt. Suffering from anoraksia
nervosa, his mind suggested pertly, while he tried to tell it
to calm down. But it kept throwing up irrelevant puns,
thoughts and ideas. He knew the symptoms. It was always

like this after the run of a show. A slow process of unwinding when the brain kept working overtime and took longer than the body to relax.

The body was doing well; it appreciated the holiday. Clachenmore was a beautiful place, though it hardly seemed worth putting on the map, it was so small. Apart from a tiny cottage given the unlikely title of 'The Post Office', there was just the hotel, a solid whitewashed square with a pair of antlers over the door. Every window offered gratuitously beautiful views—up to the rich curve of the heathery hills, sideways to the woods that surrounded the burn (free fishing for residents), down over the vivid green fields to the misty gleam of Loch Fyne.

So the situation was relaxing. And being with Frances was relaxing. Arriving at a strange hotel with an ex-wife has got the naughty excitement of a dirty weekend with a non-wife, but with more security. And Frances was being very good, not talking about defining their position and not saying were they actually going to get a divorce because it wasn't easy for her being sort of half-married and half-unmarried and what chance did she have of meeting someone else well no one in particular but one did meet people, and all that. She seemed content to enjoy the current domestic idyll and not think about the future. A line from one of Hood's letters came into his mind. 'My domestic habits are very domestic indeed; like Charity I begin at home, and end there; so Faith and Hope must call upon me, if they wish to meet.'

But he did not feel relaxed. He did not mind lines of Hood flashing into his head; that was natural; it always happened after a show; but there were other thoughts that came unbidden and were less welcome. He closed his eyes and all he could see were the writhing coils of the fat grey earthworms he had dug for bait that morning. That was not good; it made him think of worms and epitaphs. What would Martin Warburton's epitaph be? He opened his eyes.

The fish seemed to have stopped biting. Earlier in the day he had a good tug on his borrowed tackle and with excitement reeled in a brown trout all of five inches long. Since his most recent experience had been of coarse fishing, he had forgotten how vigorous even tiny trout were. But since then they had stopped biting. Perhaps it was the weather. Or he was fishing in the wrong place.

Even with the rain distorting its surface, the pool where he was did not look deep enough to contain anything very large. But there were supposed to be salmon there. So said Mr Pilch from Coventry who came up to Clachenmore every summer with the family and who liked to pontificate in the lounge after dinner. 'Oh yes, you want to ask Tam the gamekeeper about that. Actually, he's not only the game-keeper, he's also the local poacher. Only been working on the estate for about five years, but he knows every pool of that burn. Good Lord, I've seen some monster salmon he's caught. They put them in the hotel deep-freeze. Mind you . . .' Here he had paused to attend to his pipe, an aluminium and plastic device that looked like an important but inexplicable electronic component. He had unscrewed something and squeezed a spongeful of nicotine into the coal-bucket. 'Mind you, what you mustn't do is ask *how* Tam catches the fish. Oh no, I believe there are rules in fishing circles. But, you know, he goes through the water in these waders stalking them, and he can tell the pools they're in—don't know how he does it, mind—and he's got these snares and things, and his ripper. It's a sort of cord with a lot of treble hooks on. Well, he whips them out of the water on to the bank and then gets the Priest out—you know why it's called the Priest? It gives the fish their last rites. Vicious little device it is, short stick with a weighted end. Anyway, down this comes on the fish's head and that's another for the deep-freeze. Highly illegal, but highly deli-cious, eh?'

However the salmon were playing hard to get. So were the trout. So, come to that, were any fresh water shrimps that might be around. Obviously the recommended bunch of worms on a large hook ledgered to the bottom was an insufficient inducement. Charles turned to Frances, and put on his schoolboy party-piece voice. 'A recitation—*The Angler's Farewell* by Thomas Hood.

> "Not a trout there be in the place,
> Not a Grayling or Rud worth the mention,
>   And although at my hook
>   With *attention* I look
> I can ne'er see my hook with *a Tench on*!"'

Frances clapped and he bowed smugly. 'IthangyouIthangyou, and for my next trick, I was thinking of going for a walk to work off some of Mrs Parker's enormous breakfast in anticipation of her no doubt enormous lunch. Do you want to come?'

'I'm nearly at the end of this book actually and I'm quite cosy.' She looked cosy, tarpaulined in P.V.C. mac and sou'wester, crouched like a garden gnome at the foot of the tree.

'O.K. What are you reading?'

'Your *Mary, Queen of Scots*.'

'Oh Lord. That's not my book. I should have given it back. Borrowed it from someone in Edinburgh. Ha, that reminds me of Anatole France.'

'Hm?'

' "Never lend books, for no one ever returns them; the only books I have in my library are those that other people have lent me." A quote.'

'I didn't know you were given to gratuitous quotation.'

'The bloke who lent me the book would have appreciated it.'

Some Victorian spirit of Nile-source-searching prompted him to go upstream towards the spring that fed the little burn. Any hopes of finding the source before lunch were soon dashed by the stream's unwillingness to get any narrower and the steepness of the gradient down which it came. Centuries of roaring water had driven a deep cleft into the rock. Tumbled boulders enclosed dark brown pools, fed from above by broad creamy torrents or silver threads of water.

The banks were muddy and the rocks he had to climb over shone treacherously. More than once he had to reach out and grasp at tussocks of grass to stop himself from slipping.

At last he came to a part of the burn that seemed quieter than the rest. There was still the rush of water, but it was muffled by trees arcing and joining overhead, which spread a green light on the scene. Here were three symmetrical round pools, neatly stepped like soup plates up a waiter's arm.

He identified the place from Mr Pilch's descriptions in the lounge after dinner. 'Some of the pools up there are incredibly deep, just worn down into the solid rock by constant water pressure. Makes you wonder whether we take sufficient notice of the potential of hydro-jet drilling, eh? Mind you, it takes a few centuries. Still, some of those pools are supposed to be twenty feet deep. Tam claims to have caught salmon up there, though I can't for the life of me imagine how they get that high. Maybe by doing those remarkable leaps you see on the tourist posters, eh?'

But Charles did not want to think about Pilch. The enclosing trees and the muffled rush of water made the place like a fairy cave. It was magical and, in a strange way, calming. Puffed by the climb, he squatted on his heels at the foot of a tree, and started to face the thoughts which regrettably showed no signs of going away.

He knew why he was restless. It was because the explanations he had formed for recent events in Edinburgh were incomplete. Now Martin Warburton was dead, that situation looked permanent. The frustration was like getting within four answers of a completed crossword and knowing from the clues that he had no hope of filling the gaps. He could put down any combination of letters that sounded reasonable, but he would not have the satisfaction of knowing he was right. And with this particular crossword, there would not be a correct solution published in the following morning's paper.

It was partly his own fault for wanting a clear-cut answer rather than the frayed ends of reality. A basic misconception, like his idea that the police were way behind on the case.

But he could not get away from the fact that the tie-up of Martin's motivations which he and the Laird had worked out was unsatisfactory. There were too many loose ends, stray facts that he had found out and still required explanations. Though the main outline was right, there were details of Martin's obsessive behaviour that were not clear.

He worked backwards. Martin's suicide demonstrated that, at least in his own mind, the boy was guilty of something. The discovery of the Nicholson Street bomb factory made it reasonable to suppose that one of the causes of his guilt was the device planted in Charles' holdall.

But what evidence was there that he was also responsible for killing Willy? Certainly in retrospect it looked likely. Martin had actually wielded the murder weapon and Rizzio was an obvious first victim in his macabre game of historical reconstruction. But if the murder was carefully planned, the actual execution was a bit random. Assuming Martin had switched the real knife for the treated one, he still had no guarantee that he would be given that one for the photo call. Willy might have been killed by another unsuspecting actor, but would that have given Martin the requisite thrill? Charles felt ignorant of how accurate a psychopath's reconstruction of events has to be for him to commit a murder; it is not a well-documented subject.

But at least he had faced the fact that he wanted to tie up the loose ends. Just for his own satisfaction. After lunch he would be organised like James Milne, sit down with a sheet of paper and make a note of all the outstanding questions of the case. Feeling happier for the decision, he set off down the hill to the hotel.

'Three days ago, you know, I wouldn't have believed it possible to eat one of Mrs Parker's lunches within gastronomic memory of Mrs Parker's breakfast, and certainly not with the prospect of Mrs Parker's dinner looming deliciously like an enemy missile on the horizon.'

Frances laughed as she watched him put away his plateful of cod and chips without signs of strain. 'It's the famous Scottish air. Sharpens the appetite.'

He took a long swallow from his second lunchtime pint of Guinness. 'Did you finish the book?'

'Yes.'

'Good. Then you can tell me. I want some details about the Earl of Bothwell.'

'All right.' She sat expectant, her schoolmistress mind confident of its recently acquired knowledge.

'Well, we know Bothwell killed Darnley by blowing him up at Holyrood. What I want to—'

'We don't know any such thing. Holyrood's still standing. The house where Darnley was staying, the one that was blown up, was in the Kirk o'Field. And anyway, Darnley wasn't blown up; he was strangled.'

'Really.' Charles took it in slowly. 'Then what about the murder of David Rizzio? Bothwell didn't do it on his own, I know. Who was with him on the—'

'Bothwell wasn't involved in the murder of David Rizzio. Really, Charles, I thought you had a university education.'

'A long time ago. And I read English.'

'All the same. My fourth formers could do better. Rizzio was savagely murdered by Lord Darnley, Patrick Lord Ruthven (who rose from his sick bed), Andrew Ker of Fawdonside, George Douglas, um . . .' Her new store-house of information ran out.

'Really?' said Charles, even more slowly. 'Really.' Martin had read History at Derby. If he were in the grip of psychopathic identification with an historical character, surely he would at least get the facts of his obsession correct. Charles began to regret the glibness with which he had assumed that Willy's death and the bomb were automatically connected.

'Hello. Everything all right?' Mr Parker, who owned the hotel and was owned by Mrs Parker, appeared at their table

164

with the glass of whisky that was a permanent extension of his hand.

Charles and Frances smiled. 'Yes, thank you,' he said, tapping a stomach that surely could not take many more of these enormous meals without becoming gross. 'Excellent.'

'Good, good.'

'Can I top that up for you, Mr Parker?'

'Well . . . if you're having one.'

'Why not? I'll have a malt.'

'Mrs Paris?'

'No, I'll—'

'Go on.'

'All right.'

It started to rain again heavily. Long clean streaks of water dashed against the window panes. It was cosy over the whisky.

Charles proposed a toast. 'To Stella Galpin-Lord, without whom we wouldn't be here.'

'Stella Galpin-Lord,' said Mr Parker, and chuckled. 'Yes, Stella Galpin-Lord.'

'You know her well?'

'She's been here four or five times. Stella the Snatcher we nickname her.'

'Snatcher?'

'Oh, I'm sorry. Perhaps she's a friend of . . .'

'No,' said Charles in a mischievous way to encourage indiscretion.

'Well, we call her the Snatcher, short for cradle-snatcher. Let's say that when she comes here it tends to be with a young man.'

'The same young man?'

'No. That's the amusing thing. Always books as Mr and Mrs Galpin-Lord, but, dear oh dear, she must think we're daft or something. I mean, I can't believe they're all called Galpin-Lord.'

'It is a fairly unusual name.'

Mr Parker chuckled. 'It's not our business to pry. I mean,

I don't care about people's morals and that, but I must confess Mrs Parker and I do have a bit of a giggle about the Mr and Mrs Galpin-Lords.' He realised that this sounded like a lapse of professional etiquette. 'Not of course that we make a habit of laughing at our guests.'

'No, of course not,' Charles reassured smoothly. 'But you say it's always younger men?'

'Yes, actors all of them, I think. Mutton with a taste for lamb, eh? Sorry, I shouldn't have said that.'

'Hmm. And thanks to her latest actor getting a job, here we are.'

'Yes.'

'All the more reason to toast her in gratitude. Stella Galpin-Lord.'

Mr Pilch edged over from the table where Mrs Pilch and the little Pilches were finishing their apricot crumble. 'Oh, er, Mr Paris. Tam the gamekeeper's going to take me up the burn to see if we can bag a salmon. With the right sort of fly, of course.' He winked roguishly at this. 'I wondered if you fancied coming . . .?'

But Charles felt rather full of alcohol for a fishing trip. And besides, he wanted to start writing things down on bits of paper. 'No thanks. I think I'll have a rest this afternoon.'

'Perhaps there'll be another chance.' Mr Pilch edged away.

'Sure to be, Mr Paris,' whispered Mr Parker confidentially. 'I'll ask Tam to take you another day. See what you can get. Actually, when our Mrs Galpin-Lord was here last summer, she went off with Tam and they got a fifteen-pounder. Not bad.'

'And did the current Mr Galpin-Lord go with them?'

'Oh no.' Mr Parker laughed wickedly. 'I daresay he was sleeping it off. Eh?'

The rest of the afternoon seemed to lead automatically to making love, which, except for the Clachenmore Hotel's snagging brushed nylon sheets, was very nice. 'You know,' murmured Frances sleepily, 'we do go very well together.'

166

He gave a distracted grunt of agreement.

'Do you think we could ever try again?'

Another grunt, while not completely ruling out the idea, was not quite affirmative.

'Otherwise we really ought to get divorced or something. Our position's so vague.' But she did not really sound too worried, just sleepy.

'I'll think about it,' he lied. He did not want to think about the circle of going back to Frances again and things being O.K. for a bit and then getting niggly and then him being unfaithful again and her being forgiving again and and and. . . . He must think about it at some stage, but right now there were more important things on his mind.

The lunchtime alcohol had sharpened rather than blunted his perception and he was thinking with extraordinary clarity. The whole edifice of logic he had created had been reduced to rubble and a new structure had to be put up, using the same bricks, and some others which had previously been discarded as unsuitable.

Thinking of the two crimes as separate made a new approach possible. Blurred and apparently irrelevant facts came into sharp focus. Red herrings changed their hue and turned into lively silver fish that had to be caught.

It came back again to what Willy was doing over the few days before he died. The melodrama with Anna and subsequent events had pushed that line of enquiry out of his mind, but now it became all-important and the unexplained details that he had discovered were once more significant pieces in his jigsaw.

He slipped quietly out of the brushed nylon sheets without disturbing the sleeping Frances, then dressed and padded downstairs to the telephone in the hotel lobby.

First he got on to directory enquiries. Then he took a deep breath, picked up the phone again and dialled the operator. London could not be dialled direct, which made his forthcoming imposture more risky, but he could not think of another way. By the time he got through, the Clachenmore operator, the London operator, Wanewright the Merchant Bankers' receptionist and Lestor Wanewright's secretary had all heard the assumed Glaswegian tones of Detective-Sergeant McWhirter. If it ever came to an enquiry by the real police, there was a surfeit of witnesses to condemn Charles Paris for impersonating a police officer.

Fortunately Lestor Wanewright did not show any sign of suspicion. When the Detective-Sergeant explained that, in the aftermath of the deaths in Edinburgh, he was having to check certain people's alibis as a matter of routine, the young merchant banker readily confirmed Anna's statement. They had been sharing his flat in the Lawnmarket from Sunday 4th August when they had arrived back from Nice until Tuesday 13th August when he'd had to go back to work again. Yes, they had slept together over that period. Charles Paris felt a slight pang at the thought of Anna, but Detective-Sergeant McWhirter just thanked Mr Wanewright for his co-operation.

Charles stayed by the phone after the call, thinking. He had two independent witnesses to the fact that Willy Mariello had slept with a woman at his home during the three or four days before his death. Jean Mariello had spoken of blonde hairs on the pillow and she had no reason for making that up. And, according to Michael Vanderzee, Willy had called goodbye to someone upstairs when dragged off to rehearsal on the Monday before he died.

True, Willy's sex life was free-ranging and the woman might have been anyone. But Charles could only think of one candidate with, if not blonde, at least blonded hair, and a taste for younger men.

It was nothing definite, but he still felt guilty about Martin's death. If there was anything that invited investigation, he owed it to the boy's memory to investigate it.

With sudden clarity, Charles remembered the first time he had seen Willy Mariello, on the afternoon of his death. He saw again the tall figure striding ungraciously into the Masonic Hall. Followed a few moments later by Stella

Galpin-Lord, who was sniffing. Had she been crying? The memory seemed to be dragged up from years ago, not just a fortnight. But it was very distinct. He remembered the woman's face contorted with fury in the Hate Game.

That decided him. He picked up the phone again and asked for an Edinburgh number.

At first there seemed to be a crossed line, a well-spoken middle-aged woman's voice cutting across James Milne's, but it cleared and the two men could hear each other distinctly. 'James, I've been thinking again about some aspects of the case.'

'Really. So have I.'

'It doesn't all fit, does it?'

'I think most of it does.' The Laird's voice sounded reluctant. He and Charles had worked out a solution that was intellectually satisfying and he did not want their results challenged. It was the schoolmaster in him, the academic hearing that his theory has just been superseded by a publication from another university.

'You may be right, James. But for my own peace of mind, there are one or two people I'd just like to check a few details with. So I'm coming back to Edinburgh.'

'Ah. And you're asking me to put my Dr Watson hat back on?'

'If you don't mind.'

'Delighted. You'll stay here, of course?'

'Thank you.'

'When are you arriving?'

'Don't know exactly. It'll be tomorrow some time. As you know, I'm out here at Clachenmore and getting back involves a taxi to Dunoon, ferry across the Clyde to Gourock, bus to Glasgow and God knows what else. So don't expect me till late afternoon.'

'Fine. And you'll tell me all then?'

'Exactly. Cheerio.'

Then something odd happened. Charles heard the phone

put down the other end twice. There were two separate clicks.

Two separate clicks—what the hell could that mean? He was about to dismiss it as a vagary of the Scottish telephone system when a thought struck him. There were two extensions of the same telephone at Coates Gardens, one in the Laird's flat and one in the hall. Perhaps what he had taken to be a crossed line at the beginning of the call had been someone answering the downstairs telephone. And the first click was that person putting their receiver down. In other words, someone could have heard all of the conversation.

Only one woman likely to be in Coates Gardens had a middle-aged voice.

The journey to Edinburgh developed another complication when he tried to order a taxi. The only firm for miles was in Tighnabruaich and there was a funeral there the following morning which was going to appropriate every car; they could not get one to the Clachenmore Hotel until half past two in the afternoon.

There was nothing to be done about it. It just meant another morning's fishing and another of Mrs Parker's gargantuan lunches. There were worse fates.

The next morning was very, very wet. Rain fell as if God had upturned a bottomless bucket. Frances decided that she would not venture out; she curled up on the sofa in the Lounge with *Watership Down*.

'What do you think about fishing?' Charles asked, hoping Mr Parker's reply would excuse him from going out.

'Yes, not bad weather for it.'

Damn. Charles started to pull on his anorak. 'Actually,' Mr Parker continued, 'Tam was asking if I thought you'd like to go after some salmon.'

That sounded a lot more attractive than pulling worms out of damp clods in the hope of another five-inch trout. 'Really? Is he about?'

'Was earlier. There was a phone call for him. I'll see.'

Tam was found and was more than willing to conduct a guided tour of the salmon pools (no doubt in anticipation of a substantial tip). His only reservation, which Mr Parker interpreted to Charles, was that he did not approve of women being involved in fishing, and did Mrs Paris want to come? Charles set his mind at rest on that point, and then took stock of his guide.

The gamekeeper was a man of indeterminate age and impenetrable accent. His face was sucked inwards and shrivelled like perished rubber. He wore a flat cap and a once-brown overcoat with large pockets on the outside (and no doubt even larger ones on the inside).

Tam's mouth opened and uttered strange Scottish sounds which might have been asking if Charles was ready to go straight away.

'Yes,' he hazarded. 'Will I need a rod?'

Tam laughed derisively. Legal fishing methods were obviously a myth created for the tourists.

They set off, following the burn up the hill. Conversation was limited. Tam would occasionally comment on things they passed (a dead sheep, for example) and all Charles' acting skill would be required to choose the right 'Yes', 'Really?', 'Too true', 'Did they indeed?' or omnipurpose grunt. He did not have the confidence to initiate subjects himself, reacting was safer. Mr Pilch's words came back to him. 'They're a proud lot, the locals. Oh yes, you have to be careful what you say. And they have this great loyalty to their masters. In many ways, it's still an almost feudal society. Very poor though, I'm afraid. Not a lot of jobs available round here. It'll change of course when the oil comes—if it comes, which heaven forbid. You know there are plans to put up platforms just outside Loch Fyne? I hope they don't ruin the West Coast. Eh?'

None of that offered very promising conversational topics. What's it like being proud? Or living in a feudal society? Are you really very poor? What is your feeling about the proposed development of natural oil resources off the West

Coast of Scotland? Somehow none of these seemed quite the right question to ask Tam, and fortunately the gamekeeper did not appear to find the silence irksome.

At last he indicated that they had reached their destination. It was the linked series of pools where Charles had been the day before. Again the trees overhead changed the note of the running stream and the heavy dripping of rain was muffled.

'Do the salmon really get up this far?'

Tam managed to communicate that they certainly did. He had got a twenty-pounder out a good half mile farther up into the hills.

'Whereabouts do they go? Do we just look for them swimming about in the pools?'

Apparently not. In these conditions they lay still just under the bank. The skill was to spot them and whip them out of the water quickly. Tam would demonstrate.

They edged slowly down the slippery rocks to the water's edge. As they drew closer, the noise of the water increased. Swollen by rain, the cataracts pounded down on the rocks below. It was easy to see how the deep cleft had been worn down into the rock over the years.

Silently and efficiently, Tam lay down on the rocks at the waterside and peered into the bubbling green depths.

'Anything?' Charles hissed and was reprimanded by a finger on Tam's lips. The gamekeeper slid crabwise along the rocks, still looking down. Then he froze for a moment and got up.

'Big one,' he whispered. Either Charles was getting used to the accent or it was clearer close to.

'Where?'

'Directly under that rock. Have a look. But be quiet and don't move suddenly.'

Charles eased himself down to a kneeling position and, with his hands gripping the slimy edge of the pool, moved his head slowly out over the water.

At that moment his left hand slipped. It saved his life. As

his body lurched sideways, he saw the flash of the brass head of Tam's Priest as it came down. The blow aimed to the skull landed with agonising force on Charles's shoulder.

The shock of the attack stunned him even more than its violence. For a moment he lay there, the rocks hard under his back, his hair soaked with spray from the pounding water just below. Then he saw Tam advancing towards him with the Priest again upraised.

The gamekeeper must have thought he had knocked his victim out; he was unprepared for the kick in the stomach that Charles managed from his prone position. Tam staggered back clutching himself, reeled for a moment at the water's edge, then fell safely on to the rocks.

Charles had one aim, which was to get the hell out of the place. Winding his assailant had given him the opportunity. He scrambled manically over the slimy rocks, grabbing at tussocks and branches to heave himself up the gradient. His right arm screeched with pain like a gear lever in a broken gearbox. But he was getting away.

He turned for a moment. Tam was standing now, but Charles had the start. Then he saw something whip out and uncoil from the gamekeeper's hand. As the treble hooks bit into his leg and he felt the inexorable pull down towards the boiling cauldron below, Charles knew it was the ripper.

CHAPTER FOURTEEN

O'er all there hung a shadow and a fear;
A sense of mystery the spirit daunted,
And said, as plain as whisper in the ear,
The place is Haunted!

THE HAUNTED HOUSE

IN THE TRAIN from Glasgow to Edinburgh Charles said a little prayer of thanks, and reflected how frustrating it must be for God only to be in demand in times of danger, like a brilliant tap-dancer waiting for tap-dancing to come back into fashion. Still, God had saved his life and Charles Paris was suitably grateful.

There was no other explanation than divine intervention. The pain from his shoulder and the long furrows gouged in his left leg made the scene hard to forget. He could see the bank slipping past him as he was dragged painfully down to the water. He could feel the kick in the stomach with which Tam had immobilised him, and see the Priest again raised for a blow that was not going to miss.

And then, as Charles closed his eyes and vainly attempted to put his mental affairs in order, the threat vanished. Almost literally. The blow seemed a long time coming, so he crept one eye open. And Tam had disappeared.

The gamekeeper's foot must have slipped on the rocks and, caught off balance, he had fallen into the water. The force of the stream had swept him over the ledge of one pool and into the next, where he floated round like a giant face-cloth with a bubble of air caught in it.

Charles had tried to disengage the ripper from his leg, but the pain was too great, so he used a long stick to guide the body to the water's edge. Then, using both arms (though the right one felt as if it was being severed from his torso with a blowlamp), he had heaved the sodden mass on to the bank.

To his amazement, he found that Tam was still alive, unconscious, but with a strong heartbeat and pulse. Rediscovering a scrap of knowledge that had lain dormant since some aunt had given him a Boy Scout diary in his teens, Charles turned the body over and, after working the shoulders for a few minutes, was rewarded by a flow of water from the injured man's mouth. He then reckoned it was safe to leave Tam there; there was no danger of either death or escape. The body was propped up against a mossy bank and Charles started his painful course back to the hotel.

Mr Parker took control with instant efficiency. Suddenly Clachenmore did not seem so isolated. A doctor was summoned and a party of local forestry workers who were in the bar went off to fetch Tam.

The doctor did not comment on the story of two men slipping on the bank, Tam falling into the water and Charles getting tangled in the hooks and banging his shoulder on a rock; he just got on with the job. Removing the barbs of the hooks was the worst bit, but he was used to it. He explained that a pair of pliers was an essential part of a doctor's equipment in that area, though most of the hooks he came across tended to be lodged in the cheeks of people walking behind over-enthusiastic fly-fishermen. Treble hooks, he admitted, were trickier, but the principle was the same—push the hook through until its barb stood clear of the flesh, snip it off with the pliers, and then work the remains of the hook out. While this excruciating operation was conducted, Charles made a rash vow that he would give up fishing; he had never thought what it felt like for the fish before.

In spite of the pain they caused, the scrapes on his leg were not deep. The highest one needed a couple of stitches, but the others were just cleaned and dressed. The shoulder presented even less problem. There was nothing broken, just

175

severe bruising. The doctor strapped it into a sort of sling and went to tend the still-unconscious Tam, who had just been brought back.

Charles was patched up in time for lunch. Frances sat opposite him, looking anxious, but respecting his promise to explain everything in detail when it was over. There was an atmosphere of shock in the dining-room. Even Mr Pilch was subdued and did not get far pontificating to his children on Stone Age relics in Argyll.

At two thirty the taxi had arrived and, against doctor's orders and Frances' advice, Charles had started the journey to Edinburgh. Which was why he was sitting in the train, thanking God and asking God if He could see fit to spare a little more protection for the confrontation to come.

Stella Galpin-Lord had recommended Clachenmore. She knew Tam. By the attempt on Charles' life, she had nailed her colours to the mast, but it was a mast that only Charles Paris could see, and she thought Charles Paris was dead. His best weapon was going to be surprise.

She did look surprised to see him when he found her at the Masonic Hall. She had just given her nightly pep-talk to the cast of *A Midsummer Night's Dream* (which now only had three more revisualised performances to run; then in the third week of the Festival *Mary, Queen of Sots* took over). After Clachenmore Charles found it strange to think in terms of dates again. He reminded himself that it was now Thursday 29th August.

'Stella. I'd like to talk.'

'Certainly. I must say, this is a surprise. I thought we'd seen the last of you when you went to Clachenmore.'

'Yes,' he said grimly.

'Didn't you like it there?'

'There were . . . things I didn't like.'

They went to the pub near the Hall where they had last met. She had another of her vodka and Camparis; he had a large Bell's. The pain from his patched-up wounds made

176

concentration difficult, but he did not intend to talk for long.

Stella raised her glass. 'Well, this is an unexpected pleasure.'

'I want to talk about Willy Mariello.'

The brusque statement took her completely off her guard. She blushed under her make-up, and lowered the glass as if she were afraid she might drop it. 'Willy Mariello?' she echoed stupidly. 'But he's dead.'

'Yes. As you well know, he's dead.' She mouthed at him, unable to form words. 'And, Stella, I think his death may have something to do with what he was doing in the few days before he died.'

'It was an accident,' she croaked. 'It couldn't have been anything to do with—'

'Couldn't it? Let's just suppose for a moment it could. I have become very interested in what Willy was doing over those few days. So far all I can find out is that he did a bit of rehearsing, a bit of decorating in his house . . . and he slept with a woman other than his wife.'

The blush spread to the stringy parts of her neck the make-up had missed. 'So . . . what are you saying?'

'That you were that woman.'

'What if I was? Who do you think you are—the bloody Edinburgh Watch Committee? If two people are attracted to each other and want to sleep together, what bloody business is it of yours?'

'None at all. So when did this little affair start?'

'We met in a pub on the Saturday night. It was obvious he was attracted to me.' Charles wondered. He had a more likely vision of Willy, furious at Anna's rejection of him, on the lookout for anything, so long as it was female. 'And I went back to his house that night.'

'I see.'

Stella saw some meaning that Charles had not intended in his remark. 'I suppose you're going to say something about our age difference.'

'No, I'm not.' His own recent behaviour would make such

comment hypocritical. Anyway, it was irrelevant. 'And the affair continued for a few more nights?'

'Yes.'

'Until the Tuesday morning when he told you to get lost.'

Her eyes flashed under their lash-stretched lids. 'He did not! It was my idea. I thought it unsuitable that it should continue. I believe in love on impulse; I don't think one should be tied.'

A suitable philosophy if no one's ever tried to tie you and you have to make all the running, Charles thought. But he did not say it. 'I see. Well, thank you for telling me that. I'm sure it's something the police don't know.'

She gaped and her real age showed. 'What do you mean? Surely the police think Willy's death was an accident ...? Or, if it wasn't, that that boy Martin—'

'If it wasn't, I feel we should tell them everything we know about the few days before he died.'

'I don't think it's relevant.'

'You don't. I do. Perhaps there are other things we ought to know about the period. I mean, what *was* Willy doing?'

'Willy—he was, as you said, rehearsing and decorating. The place was full of plaster dust and paint and all kinds of rubbish. Look, Mr Paris, I'd like to know why the hell you're asking me all these questions.'

'Because, Miss Galpin-Lord, I believe that, after a quarrel with Willy Mariello, in which he probably made disparaging remarks about your looks and general appeal, you arranged for him to be killed.'

Her face crumbled until it looked of pensionable age. 'What? Murder?'

'Yes.'

'And what proof do you have of this?'

'The proof comes from the fact that when you realised I was on to you you arranged to have me murdered too. Only unfortunately Tam the gamekeeper failed in his attempt, which is why you see me here now.'

'Tam?' Her voice was very weak.

'From Clachenmore. Now, come on, you set me up to go there because you knew Tam was to hand if necessary. Don't pretend you don't know him.'

'I know who you mean, but I don't know him well.'

'Well enough to know how poor he is and what he'd be prepared to do for money.'

'But how am I supposed to have arranged this?'

'Simple. You rang him at the hotel. I know he had a call this morning.'

'Don't be ridiculous. I hardly know the man.' Now she was almost shouting.

'You've known him ever since he started working at Clachenmore.'

'I've only seen him there a couple of times.'

'Then maybe you knew him before. In his previous job. It was somewhere in the same area.'

'I didn't know him then. Not at all. I've never even been to Glenloan House.'

'Where?'

'Glenloan House.'

There was only one other person Charles had ever heard use that name, someone who once owned a house in Meadow Lane.

He moved quickly and efficiently, as if the actions he had to make were long premeditated and rehearsed.

A streetlamp outside the house in Meadow Lane showed it to be dark and empty. Fortunately, there was nobody about to see him enter. He moved towards the front door, thinking to break one of the glass panels and reach round to the catch, when a sudden memory stopped him. The window catch Jean Mariello had complained about had been forgotten in the rush of her leaving, and the sash slid up easily.

Inside he was glad of the light from the streetlamp, which gave a pale glow to the white room.

Relevant memories came back. Again he saw Willy sitting opposite him in the Truth Game, long brown hair greyed with plaster dust. He remembered Stella's repetition of the fact that he had been decorating; Jean Mariello's words about her husband—'He'd suddenly get sick of his surroundings and want to change it all'—'Saw himself as the great landowner in his ancestral home in front of his blazing fire. The man of property.'

It was on the left. When he looked along the wall, he could see the light catch on the slight prominence of plaster where the fireplace had been filled in. There was a central heating radiator fixed to the wall across it.

The radiator swivelled on its brackets to lie nearly flat on the floor. Behind it the plaster was more uneven, as if done in haste. Even in the pale light available, it was clear that the paint over this area was newer than in the rest of the room.

He was lucky. The pile of rubble which he had noticed when he last saw Jean Mariello was still there. He found a rusty screwdriver and started to chip away at the new plaster.

Willy had made the task easier by the slapdash way in which he had replaced the bricks. As he flaked off plaster and dug into the mortar, Charles tried to visualise the scene. Willy Mariello, the spoilt child, saw things going against him. The group had split up. His new career as an actor was not going to lead to instant stardom. His marriage was in shreds and Anna had rejected him. Bored and frustrated, he suddenly decided he was sick of his house. Where was the fireplace he had dreamed of?—replaced by bloody central heating. It would be a big job to change it. But Willy was impulsive; he did not like to go the boring correct way about things. Smash the fireplace covering first, and then see if he liked it.

But something had made him decide to fill the space in again. Charles prised away one brick, but the light did not reach the void. If only he had a torch. He began to be acutely conscious of the pain in his shoulder as he drove the screwdriver into the recalcitrant mortar. He was sweating.

He had to remove six bricks before he could see anything

in the space. But as the sixth was worked out of its socket, the light flowed in and he shared the revulsion that Willy Mariello must have felt at the discovery. In spite of the discoloration of dirt and time and the decay of the fabric of the trousers and sock, what he saw had once been a human leg.

Nausea rising in his throat, he made himself confirm the initial impression. But there was no doubt. He found flesh dried down on to bone. It seemed that there was a complete body in the fireplace.

Again his movements were automatic. As he rose he realised how long he had been kneeling on the floor. The pain burned in his tattered leg. He decided to use the front door.

As he opened it, a large block of stone from the portico crashed down in front of him. It was the slab carved with the date. 1797. If he had not remembered the faulty catch and broken into the house the obvious way, it would have killed him.

CHAPTER FIFTEEN

At last he shut the ponderous tome,
  With a fast and fervent clasp
He strain'd the dusky covers close,
  And fixed the brazen hasp :
"Oh, God ! could I so close my mind,
  And clasp it with a clasp !"

THE DREAM OF EUGENE ARAM

JAMES MILNE OPENED the door of his flat. 'Ah,' he said.
It was not an expression of surprise, just an acknowledge-
ment of information received. 'Won't you come in?'

'Thank you.'

'Malt?'

'Thank you.' It was exactly as before, both sitting in their
comfortable chairs with their glasses of malt whisky, surrounded by books.

'I heard you had arrived in Edinburgh from one of the
Derby students.'

'Yes. I know you knew I was here.'

The Laird understood. 'You've been to Meadow Lane?'

'Yes. As you see, the slab missed me. One of your little
plans that didn't work.'

'Ah well.' The man did not seem emotional, just tired.
'After that, I'm surprised you came round here on your own.'

'You mean the malt could be poisoned or you could have
a gun hidden somewhere?'

'It's possible.'

'No. That's not your style. The method must be indirect,
done without you present. Then you can just shut your mind
to the fact that it ever happened, and go back to your books.'

'You seem to understand me very well, Charles.'

'I think I do. Various things you said. Something about envying a writer his ability to live by remote control.'

'Yes. And you said writing wasn't like that.'

'It isn't.'

The Laird chuckled, as if their old conviviality had been re-established. Then he was silent for a moment. 'Right, how much do you know?'

'Just about everything. As you see from my face and hands, I've been dismantling a wall.'

An expression of pain cut across Milne's face. 'So you've seen it?'

'Just as Willy Mariello did.'

'Yes. He came and told me on the morning before he died.'

'And did he say he was going to the police?'

'No, no, that wasn't his idea at all. He suggested that I was a wealthy man and . . .'

'Blackmail. That would fit everything I've heard of Willy. And sort out his mortgage arrears. He could live off you for the rest of his life.'

'I don't know. That's what he suggested. Regular payments or . . .'

'He'd go to the police.' The Laird nodded. 'And that was why you had to kill him.'

There was a slight hesitation before a muttered 'Yes.'

'Who was it, James?'

The man looked flustered and pathetic. 'No one. It was . . . just someone I knew . . . a . . . no one . . .'

'Who?'

'A boy. From the school. From Kilbruce. A pupil of mine. He was called . . . Lockhart.' The Laird put his words together with difficulty. 'He was a good boy. I liked him. He seemed interested in my books and . . . He . . . used to come round for tea or . . . That was all, really. In spite of what they said, that was all.

'Then one evening he came round . . . he wasn't in school uniform . . . and he said he was going to run away to

London, and he'd left a note at school and sent one to his parents. I said I thought it was foolish, but I couldn't stop him. And that . . . I'd miss him . . . Just that, nothing more.

'But when I said it, he said something . . . vile . . . a comment on why I'd miss him. He said . . . it was just like all the others . . . that I . . . It wasn't true!' His hands were kneading the arms of his chair rapaciously. 'I don't know what happened then. I . . . he was dead. Perhaps I strangled him, I don't know. But suddenly he was dead.

'Then I knew I had to get rid of the body. The men had just finished installing the central heating. I thought of the fireplace. There were no development plans for the area. The house wouldn't be demolished, and no one was going to revert to open fires after central heating had been put in.' (No one except an impulsive fool like Willy Mariello, Charles reflected wryly.) 'It'd never be found out while I was alive, and there was nobody to mind when I was dead. So that's what I did.'

'And everyone assumed the boy had gone to London as he said, and disappeared?'

'Yes. You keep reading of cases of kids doing that.'

There was a long pause. 'And you managed to live in the house and forget it?'

'Yes. It had been so quick. Sometimes I really thought it hadn't happened, that I'd read about it in a book or . . . I didn't think about it.'

'Just as you wouldn't have thought about me if Tam had drowned me or if that piece of masonry had crushed my skull.'

'Exactly,' he said with engaging honesty. 'I've always found it difficult to believe in the reality of other people. You know, I like them, but if I don't see them, it's as if they'd never existed. Except my mother, she was real.'

His eyes glazed over and Charles pulled him roughly back on to the subject. 'Right. So we know why you had to kill Willy Mariello.'

'Yes. The dagger was just a trial run, really. I never

thought it would work. But I saw them downstairs at lunchtime on Tuesday and thought that'd do until I found a better way. There was a long chance it might work.' A gleam of intellectual satisfaction came into his eye. 'And it did. The perfect remote control crime.'

'Yes,' said Charles wryly. 'And then I rather played into your hands by confiding in you as my Dr Watson.'

'You did. At least it made me fairly certain that I wasn't on your list of suspects. That is, until the middle of last week.'

'Why? What happened then?'

'You started getting evasive, which seemed odd. I felt you were holding something back. But what really scared me was when you said you were going to give the case up, because it involved someone you knew well. I thought you were on to me then.'

'Good God. That wasn't what I meant at all. I was talking about Anna. You know, I told you I was having an affair with her. Well, at that stage I was suspicious of her.'

'Oh.' The Laird sounded disappointed. 'Then I needn't have planted the bomb.'

'It was you!' Charles sat bolt upright in his chair.

'Yes. I'd been building up your suspicions of Martin Warburton to keep the heat off me anyway. But I did follow him and I actually managed to break into the Nicholson Street flat. When I saw all the bomb-making equipment I knew it might be useful. Martin seemed in such a bad state that he wouldn't be able to give a coherent account of his movements. So when I thought you were on to me, I picked up the bomb and waited my chance. Once it was planted, all I had to do was stay with you until it was discovered and you'd cease to be suspicious of me. The fact that it happened at Holyrood just added drama to the situation.'

'So the break in the connection was deliberate? You knew the thing wouldn't blow up?'

The Laird nodded smugly, pleased with his own cunning. Charles began to realise just how detached the man's intellectual processes had become from his emotional reactions. For him life was an elaborate mental game, in which passion was an intruder. The Laird expanded on his plot. 'And then of course Martin Warburton played into my hands completely. I knew he was in a confused state, but suicide was more than I could have hoped for. It made the whole thing cut and dried, a complete case with a problem and an unquestionable solution. And, from my point of view, a perfect sequence of crimes, which neither I nor anyone else need ever have thought about again.

'And if you hadn't worked it all out at Clachenmore, or even if Tam (who incidentally was my mother's gamekeeper for years and would do anything for me) had made a clean job of dispatching you, it would have worked.' Charles was again amazed by the detached way in which the man could talk to someone he had twice tried to murder. The Laird went on in the same level tone. 'By the way, what was it made you sure it was me?'

'Ah, well . . .' Charles was damned if he was going to admit the circuitous route by which he had reached the solution. And then suddenly his mind joined two incidents whose significance he should have seen long before. *'The Dream of Eugene Aram,'* he pronounced confidently.

'What?'

'Hood's poem. When you returned my book, I asked if you had read it and you said "No", quite vehemently. But then later you quoted from the poem . . .'

The Laird supplied the words as if in a trance.

' "Much study had made him very lean
And pale and leaden-eyed." '

Charles nodded, confident in his lies. 'So that made me wonder why you wanted to divert my attention from *Eugene Aram*. I looked back at the poem and there it was—the story of a schoolmaster who committed a murder and was not found out for many years until the body was discovered. Obviously you didn't want to set my mind on that track.'

The Laird agreed tonelessly. 'I didn't think you'd noticed.'

'Ah,' said Charles with what he hoped was subtle intonation. And then he quoted from *The Dream of Eugene Aram*.

> ' "Then down I cast me on my face,
>   And first began to weep,
> For I knew my secret then was one
>   That earth refused to keep :
> Or land or sea, though he should be
>   Ten thousand fathoms deep.
>
> So wills the fierce avenging Sprite,
>   Till blood for blood atones !
> Ay, though he's buried in a cave,
>   And trodden down with stones,
> And years have rotted off his flesh,—
>   The world shall see his bones !" '

'I see. And that's what made you suspicious ?'

Charles had not the hypocrisy to say yes; he let the silence stand. James Milne did not seem to mind. On the contrary, he looked serene, almost pleased at the literary resolution of his case.

There was a long silence, during which he refilled their glasses. Then he sat back in his chair and took a long swallow. 'The question now is, Charles, what happens next ?'

'Yes.'

'I suppose you feel bound to go to the police ?' There was a hint of pleading in his tone, but Charles ignored it.

'Yes, James, I'm afraid I do. Not because I hate you or anything like that. As I said to you once, I have a stereotyped view of murderers as wicked people I dislike. You don't fit that. I like you and I'm sorry to have to do this.

'I'm not even particularly shocked by some of your crimes. I don't know about the boy, what the rights and wrongs were, but that sounds like a moment of passion, a sudden burst of insanity that could happen to any of us given the right sort of provocation. I don't even mind that much about Willy Mariello. He was a slob whom nobody seems to have mourned. And, as for your attacks on me, they were a logical consequence of your position and my actions.

'But, James, I can't ever forgive you for the crime you didn't commit—Martin Warburton's suicide. That boy was mixed up beyond belief. But he was very talented and at a difficult time in his life. He needed help. What you did by your elaborate framing of him was to put the boy under pressures that few people completely in control of their senses could manage. I know you didn't think about him as a person; he was just a counter in your game of self-concealment. And it's because you didn't think of him as a person that I regard you as a dangerous man, who should probably be put away.'

There was another silence. James Milne did not look shattered, like a man whose life had just been ruined, but piqued, like a debater who had just lost a point. He rose with a sigh. 'Perhaps we should go to the police then.'

'I think we should.'

'I'll take a book.' He turned round to the shelves and instinctively found a leather-bound copy of Oscar Wilde's *De Profundis*. 'I dare say there'll be a lot of sitting around at the police station.'

'Yes,' said Charles, 'I dare say there will.'

CHAPTER SIXTEEN

My temples throb, my pulses boil,
  I'm sick of Song, and Ode, and Ballad—
So, Thyrsis, take the Midnight Oil
  And pour it on a lobster salad.
                    TO MINERVA—FROM THE GREEK

CHARLES SPENT a lot of time with the police over the
next couple of days and did not make it back to Clachenmore. Frances joined him in Edinburgh on the Sunday.
They booked into the Aberdour Guest House, where Mrs
Butt patently did not think they were married.

Frances wanted to get back to London to prepare for the
new school term, but Charles persuaded her to stay till the
Tuesday morning so that they could attend the first night of
Mary, Queen of Sots. His stay at the Festival would not be
complete without that. He also managed to fit in a visit to
Lesley Petter, who was cheerful at the prospect of leaving
the Infirmary in a couple of days.

On the Monday they arrived at the Masonic Hall at
seven, half an hour before the show was due to start, to find
Pam Northcliffe and others energetically piling up the chairs
from the back part of the hall. They were watched by an
unamused group of young men in tracksuits.

'Pam, what's going on?'

'Oh Lord, Charles, hello. There's been the most frightful
cock-up, I'm afraid. This lot say they're booked in here for
badminton on Monday nights. Apparently it was only
cancelled for the two weeks and they aren't going to budge.'

'Whose fault is it?'

'Brian Cassells booked it.'

189

'Say no more. Where is he? Surely he should be flashing his dinner jacket and sorting it out.'

'Oh, he's gone.'

'Gone?'

'Yes, he got the Civil Service job he was after, so he's gone to have a holiday in Italy before it starts.'

'Tell me, which Ministry is the job in?'

'Social Services, I think. He'll be doing pensions.'

That seemed apt. There was some justice after all. Charles could visualise a glowing career for Brian withholding money from old ladies.

'So is the performance off?'

'Oh no. The show must go on. Sam says so,' Pam announced with pride.

'Why? Is Sam directing?'

'Yes. As well as playing Rizzio and Bothwell and doing the music.'

'Where's Michael Vanderzee?'

'Ah. He had an offer to go and direct Humpe's *Gangrene* at the Almost Blue Theatre.'

'And he went?'

'Oh yes. It's a chance in a lifetime.'

'Of course.'

At that moment Sam Wasserman appeared from behind the curtains, distraught in doublet and hose. 'Pam, Pam darling, my tights have laddered.'

'Don't worry, darling, I've got a needle and thread in my bag. Oh Lord, I'd better go.'

'O.K. Good luck.' Pam bustled off, blushing. Charles decided he and Frances had time for a drink. And might need one.

They did. The audience was tiny. Brian Cassells' theory about morbid publicity being good publicity had proved incorrect and the average Edinbourgeois was too affronted by the title alone to consider seeing the show. The atmosphere in the hall was not helped by the full houselights necessary for the badminton and the pounding feet and occasional curses of the players.

But ultimately it was the play that made the evening a disaster. Sam Wasserman's leaden allegories proved no more lively onstage than they had when he described them. They were presented in the metronomic blank verse that can only be produced by a Creative Writing course and were mixed with songs that provided as much contrast as a bread-filled sandwich.

Charles tensed up when Anna came on, looking very beautiful in her Tudor costume. But when she spoke, he relaxed. There was no real pang, just the impression that she was rather theatrical. She was talented, but mannered. Two years at drama school might make her quite good.

At the interval Charles and Frances snuck out to the pub, giggling like schoolchildren. And somehow they omitted to return for the second act.

On the train back to London on the Tuesday morning Charles gave Frances an edited version of the whole case. When he came to the end, she tut-tutted. 'Charles, I can't think why you've suddenly developed this very dangerous hobby. Why can't you take up golf or bowls like most middle-aged men?'

'I don't know. It's not deliberate. It's just if I get into a situation I have to find out what happened, find out the truth, I suppose.'

'Well, you did in this case.'

'Yes. Mind you, I took my time. I think I must have barked up every tree in the park before I found one with anyone in it.'

At King's Cross Underground Station they paused for a moment, slightly embarrassed. Then Charles kissed Frances goodbye. She caught the Northern Line to Highgate and he caught the Circle Line to Bayswater.